FOOZLERS

OTHER WORKS BY TOM OSBORNE

Under the Shadow of Thy Wings
9 Love Poems
Please Wait for Attendant to Open Gate
The Reamer's Car Club Blues Band Story
Tenth Avenue Bike Race (Johnny Tens)

Foozlers

a novel

TOM OSBORNE

ANVIL PRESS | VANCOUVER

Foozlers
Copyright © 2004 by Tom Osborne

All rights reserved. No part of this book may be reproduced by any means without the prior written permission of the publisher, with the exception of brief passages in reviews. Any request for photocopying or other reprographic copying of any part of this book must be directed in writing to ACCESS: The Canadian Copyright Licensing Agency, One Yonge Street, Suite 1900, Toronto, Ontario, Canada, M5E 1E5.

NATIONAL LIBRARY OF CANADA CATALOGUING IN PUBLICATION DATA
Osborne, J. Thomas
Foozlers / Tom Osborne.

ISBN: 1-895636-64-7
I. Title
PS8589.I34G64 2004   C813'.54   C2003-907218-5

Cover illustration: Shawn Shepherd
Book design: HeimatHouse

Printed and bound in Canada

Represented in Canada by the Literary Press Group
Distributed by the University of Toronto Press

The publisher gratefully acknowledges the financial assistance of the B.C. Arts Council, the Canada Council for the Arts, and the Book Publishing Industry Development Program (BPIDP) for their support of our publishing program.

Anvil Press
P.O. Box 3008,
Main Post Office
Vancouver, B.C. V6B 3X5
CANADA
www.anvilpress.com

Foozle: to bungle; misfire

to
Miranda, Adam and Alana who have suffered well
the foozling of their elders

Against stupidity the very gods themselves
contend in vain.
— Schiller,
The Maid of New Orleans

I got to be somewhere.
— Hector Moses Lake,
Foozlers

Prologue / 9

The Perilous Journey / 11

The Crucial Struggle / 99

The Exaltation of the Heroes / 173

Glossary / 198

Prologue

August 26th
From your Father and I
in the 11th year of this absurdity.

Dear Jeremy,

I am writing to you again although your father and I both think it foolish, seeing as how we all live in the same city. We have said it many times before as you are well aware, that we realize the necessity of one's children leaving the comparative safety of the home to make their own way (as your brother and sister have so successfully done) and find their niche in life. I won't go into the worry you have caused us, of this too, you are well aware, but a mother needs to know her children, however grown up, are well. God knows your father struggles daily with the mystery of you living the way you do and takes heavily to the bottle. Forget I said that, this letter is not (as any of the others over the years) meant as a reprimand. We know you make the few miles every Christmas and are grateful to the

Powers That Be for these small mercies. Enclosed is another letter from the Loans Officer at the University requesting payment, now, I believe, seven years in arrears. I have feigned ignorance of your whereabouts as usual, much to your father's chagrin, as you know he is a man of high moral and ethical standards (the only reason he hasn't paid it himself) and I only lament the monthly coming of these statements and his taking to the bottle. But that, I am well aware, is no concern of yours. Your sister's birthday is next Tuesday I remind you, and hope you will send greetings or pay a simple visit. I must go now, things to do.

As always, Mother,
with love

P.S. Although it pains me to do so, I have decided to donate all your sporting equipment to a local Boy's Club. Let me know if there is anything you wish to keep.

The Perilous Journey

1

White and Purple Balls

HECTOR LAKE IS NOT THE NAME of a place, or a lake, but it is the name of a body of water, that is, a body mostly of water. His full name is Hector Moses Lake, the Moses being the derivative of a skimpy spattering of religious knowledge in the lives of his two hard-working working-class parents, Tia and Murray Lake, who, thirty-six years earlier at the Office of the Registrar in Boise, Idaho, suddenly felt a name from the scriptures would be fitting. It's a moment of intense spiritual confusion, near panic, the Idaho sky outside marbled ominously with slate-grey furrows of dark cloud, a storm threatening, while inside Mr. and Mrs. Lake huddled together under the impatient eyes of the office clerk and the name Moses was finally decided on by the two grasping but well-meaning imaginations. This is, then, appropriately, written, and the Lakes turn family-like to the door to begin the nurturing and raising of little snot-nosed Hector, who, cooing adoringly and wrapped in a blue flannel blanket, clutches his mother's breast and wrings his tiny hands and feet into white and purple balls.

But that was then. Now, at this precise moment thirty-six years later, the six-foot, three-and-a-half inch, two-hundred-and-thirty pound and heavily muscled body of little son Hector, heroin addict and just fresh out of jail after serving a six-month stretch, approaches the front door of Delgado's Pet Mart. Katrinna Reticuli has entered the pet store first, as planned, fabricating the death of a favourite budgie to get the store clerk's attention. It's worked only too well, the store clerk seen through the window leaning forward from the waist when hearing her story—"All too familiar the pain the death of a loved one can inflict," he's saying—he'd had, in fact, a much revered blue-naped parrot from Palawan Island in the Philippines drop dead on him only the day before. He suggests a visit to the Budgie Room, head still bowed slightly in commiseration and it's unbelievable luck as Katrinna sees the Budgie Room is closed off from the rest of the store. She follows, the clerk leading the way careful to maintain a respectable pace concerned as to the delicacy of emotions in this obviously distraught member of the fair sex.

Enter then Hector Lake, determined and drug-sick, through the front door and making his way quickly through a menagerie of snakes and lizards, kittens, bunnies and pups, brightly coloured fishes from the waters of Tobago and past the dull stare of a pygmy chimp from the Okavango Swamp of Botswana. Reaching the far wall which is shelved to the ceiling with box cages of exotic birds, his eyes are glued from the start on the only cage to hold an all-white one—*"Looks like a parrot, only bigger, and has those big feathers sticking out of its head,"* he remembers.

He does quietly acknowledge at this point what

Katrinna would acknowledge later back at the car, that this bird does look kind of big to be a baby, which is what he's supposed to be boosting, but it's time to act, and besides, baby whales are as big as a house when first born and calves come out already walking. Who knows what Nature is doing? (It will be some time later while on the nod, that he can lament his lack of a formal education and decide that having knowledge only in the intricacies of football and B&Es doesn't always cut it. He would then have known such things as: "a bird appears a thoughtless thing . . . but no doubt he has his little cares," or at the very least have been exposed to any *Field Guide to Birds of New Guinea and the Islands of Geelvink Bay*, and thus been informed that the *kakatoe qalerita triton* is equipped with "a sturdy bill and a voice of harsh, raucous screech terminating with a slight upward inflection." Or he would know enough in any event to be suspicious of the latent darkness of the soul of any bird whose practice it is to "lay their two eggs on a bed of rotten humus.")

   He opens the cage door stifling a cry of pain as a black beak clamps itself on a finger. The entire wall of cages erupts in an uproar of various squawks of alarm from the other birds. Other animals in the store join in with their own variations of calls of danger. He reacts with his other hand, managing to get it around the cockatoo's throat and throttling it enough to get it to release its hold. He had planned to just stuff the bird in his jacket but the surprise attack puts a damper on that idea and instead he crams the beating feathery mass back into the cage, latching it shut and grabbing the whole contraption in his arms and making for the back doors.

In the Budgie Room, Katrinna tenses. In her hands, a little feathered bundle of greens and blues that pecks lightly at her palm. The store clerk seems not to have noticed the outward sounds of mayhem erupting in the store but it's not without a tightening in her guts that Katrinna sees Hector Lake streaking by the doorway of the Budgie Room, a colossal birdcage full of a whirring beating whiteness in tow.

2

Wahzoo

HECTOR LAKE HAD BEGUN THE DAY in a not-unfamiliar state of heroin withdrawal with all the accompanying heebie-jeebies. Wearing blue jeans, yellow T-shirt, a ripped-off pair of ill-fitting but brand new black low-cut leather boots and a prized well-zippered jacket, also black leather. The boots are not of choice but of opportunity, the preferred footwear being Reebok NFL Game Day black and white cross-trainers, but these are not always easy to come by. At 8:45 a.m. he's attempting to wheel Jerry Lowe's rust-primered Volkswagen bug through a left-hand turn at Main Street and Terminal Avenue in Vancouver, British Columbia, and much as plagued the original Moses when finally given his orders atop the mountain, there now seems an interminable number of things for Hector Lake to do to get his mission accomplished.

He prepares, already well into the intersection and mentally listing priorities. A hand signal out the window? Optional. The shifting down of gears? Maybe not. The pumping of the brakes while keeping both hands available for battling the vibrations from the steering wheel seems more important at this point. Vehicles converge on the intersection, it seems, from all directions and through the windshield of one he can see a family of faces watching him and is sure he can read the lips of one of the kids in the back seat saying, "What's that man doing, Daddy?"

He brakes, the car not slowing. Reaching down he fishes a tattered paperback from under the brake pedal where it's fallen and wedged, *Fat City* by Leonard Gardiner. He pulls hard on the wheel still pumping the brakes. More vehicles than should be seem to converge in the intersection, signalling turns left and right. He tries the horn, the horn that he now notices—like the braking and signal lights, heater, one headlight and God knows what else—doesn't work. And he's junk-sick too, intensifying what should be a simple enough manoeuvre into one of gigantic complications.

There are some near-misses and the blasting of horns that *do* function before he realizes he's made it through the intersection and is safely on his way. He's perspiring heavily, although the morning's cool. He's a ship lost at sea in need of a fix, a position. His blood courses, he can hear it. It bubbles and swirls in his ears, predicting, and rightly, that the day was not going to be an easy one. He would have to score some dope soon.

It was not always this way. There was, when he takes the time to remember (which isn't often if he can help it), a healthier, happier time. A time to remember an up-and-coming young athlete, a highschool superstar in his own right. These remembrances are known by few, and believed on the whole to be true, even though the information does come from Hector Lake himself. They usually come in bits and pieces, after a heroin fix or a few drinks, and embellished somewhat by the whims and nuances of memory and overridden with a necessary blocking of pain. There's the talented highschool quarterback with the possibility of a spot in the college draft. At the age of eighteen the young quarterback already has a place of his own, paid for by working nights and weekends delivering pizzas in a lime-green Toyota. And he's no dummy either, averaging Bs on the academic side. There's the Big Game, scouts from the colleges rumoured to be in the stands. There's great excitement, highschool hi-jinks and frenzied pep-rallies, adoration. And, yes, possibly a few slate-grey furrows of dark cloud lancing the California sky. It's the area championship, Santa Barbara, the Idaho hills left behind some time ago by the family when the young athlete was but the tender age of six. So—the remembrance goes—it's on the surf-whipped shores of the bright blue Pacific where the young quarterback leads his team to victory and the championship, and at the final whistle, he is hoisted high and bounced off the field on the shoulders of his teammates. And it's also on the surf-whipped shores of the bright blue Pacific where lives The Woman of Great Beauty, Virginia, catching the young quarterback's eye as far back as Grade Ten, her bare knees touching one another under the desk adjacent to his in Mr. Spotlee's Social Studies class.

Now far from those playing fields of his youth, Hector Lake is being bounced again, down Broadway, having survived three more intersections in what he now refers to simply as "the shitbox." His hands are still fighting the wheel as he scouts for a convenient corner store. He is now almost twenty-four hours cold-turkey and a furrow of dark cloud can be seen rolling in from the east over the

Vancouver skyline. He pulls the shitbox over, suspicious of the windshield wipers. He flicks the switch. Nothing happens. He gets out, slamming the door, heading for a small grocer's spotted a few doors down.

A bell tinkles over his head as he enters, nostrils filled with the sickly sweet smell of decomposing fruit. A little Chinese man standing behind the counter, looking sad, as if too remembering the Big Game . . . the elation, the conspicuous absence of The Woman of Great Beauty attending the game, the young quarterback secreted under the shower after the game—drowning for the moment all sounds and fears—eyes gazing down through the wall of water, to spy, peeping out from a mat of hair, one's tiny shrivelled wahzoo.

The Chinese man slides a pack of cigarettes across the counter and Hector can't be sure if he has the right change. The sad man nods and Hector makes for the door as coins roll off the countertop and spin across the floor. Outside, the furrow of dark cloud has disappeared as he wedges himself back into the shitbox. The coach's eyes, he remembers, when they smuggled the beer in, were proud and turned away.

The house stands on a hill above the park. Across the way from the base of the hill lie the train yards, and beyond that the highrise-blocked skyline of the city set against the mountains that rise beyond that. And Hector Lake, at 9:23 a.m., junk-sick, remembering, approaches this house as he had once approached his own that time long ago, that other house where once the young quarterback had lived with The Woman of Great Beauty. Where he had once stood in another doorway just as he now stands in this one glaring at Jerry Lowe who'd lent him the car—that shitbox—although in that other time he was neither angry nor junk-sick, having up to that point never done drugs. And in this remembrance of that other house of long ago there is not a jock face to be seen or any other familiar face in the crowd filling the suite, only the face of Virginia coming forward out of the mob, two eyes burning bright, a warm beery kiss on those football hero's lips. "We're having a party," as outside the California sky is streaked with red across a growing black, the school colours, and the horizon appears as if in motion, climbing to lie with slate-grey furrows of cloud as night falls, the young quarterback soon propped in a corner of the kitchen, the shadows seeming friendlier under the kitchen cabinets. Sunrise in that other time sees excursions off to pick up more liquor, more drugs, young Hector by now a willing participant and blasted at the wheel of another Volkswagen bug, this one yellow and a convertible, this one Virginia's pride and joy. Her hair streams the warm dawn air, the top down, the world belongs to the young. And those few moments with no good, no bad. No up, no down, out carefree along the road under an endless sky—stoned, drunk, blotto and fried. And anyone could have thought the road forked, doing fifty or sixty, eyeballs glazed and driving between two power poles which turned out to be one and sounds then felt more than heard, a tragic mishap compounded no less by all the uncomprehending hells of adolescence. There's a lasting vision of the face of Virginia through a hospital glass, a mass of scars and bitterness. And there for the young quarterback everything seems forever over, from there the road only seems to wind down to the heavier stuff—ice cubes and fire—life hung out on the odd high, then crashing into power-pole lows. And at 9:25 a.m., at the house on the hill in Vancouver, British Columbia, this is one of the lows.

Jerry Lowe, of slighter build, about five-eleven in blue jeans and white oversized T-shirt and favouring high-cut brown leather civil war "snoot" boots, has jerked from the sofa seeing Hector Lake in the doorway.

"Mr. Lake."

"Mr. Lowe."

"Everything okay?"

"Found another book of yours. Out in the fucking car."

"Yeah?"

"I should kill you, you bastard, for letting me drive that pile of shit."

"That 'pile of shit', my dear fellow, is a fucking antique. Look it up on the internet."

"That 'antique' is a fucking death-trap."

"You look bad. I'll get you a drink."

Jerry Lowe moves to the kitchen. Hector Lake shoves past to the sofa and flops. A book, *The Ivory Grin* by Ross MacDonald, is kicked aside.

"Your grandmother really die on this thing?" he says but doesn't wait for an answer, and jeez-fucking-uz, but he's got the sick-man jitters bad. Ice cubes and fire. Staring at the ceiling, a water stain spread out across it that looks like a horse rearing.

He calms, then at 9:27 a.m. is raging all over again, gazing down at his ill-fitting but at least brand-new leather boots propped up on the end of the sofa, one toe all ripped to ratshit.

"What the fuck, Lowe!"

And Jerry Lowe notices the boot too, standing over Hector with a glass of whisky offered, while outside, back down among the shadows along the floor of the rust-primered shitbox where the gas pedal should be, a jagged knob pokes its steely head up from the floor, small strips of shiny black leather hanging off.

3

Felonious Simplistics

JERRY LOWE SITS ALONE IN THE rust-primered getaway car in back of Delgado's Pet Mart. This is it, the waiting has begun and with no idea for how long. And there is time to wonder with that undisclosed amount of time on his hands, what would be the immediate problems, if any. No gas gauge is an obvious one. And having to keep the engine running no matter what or for how long, the last demand made by Hector Moses Lake before he disappeared around the corner enroute to the front entrance of Delgado's Pet Mart. And how long is long? That's a good one. It would maybe be better to just limit his concerns to things under his control. Like when the time comes, the clutch work goes smoothly, knee and ankle joints well-limbered and moving in perfect synchronization. And that the motor actually remains idling, on the strength of conviction if nothing else. Give it a little gas anyway. And does the same thing happen to everybody, feeling suddenly so conspicuous sitting quietly with the motor running behind Delgado's Pet Mart, convinced that anyone passing by knows exactly what you're up to? Better still, how did he end up here in the first place?

That morning he'd been reading, stretched out on his dead grandmother's sofa. Hector had borrowed the car to go and meet someone to try and set up a score and had returned in an agitated state. After Hector Lake had calmed down about his mangled boot, all seemed to be going well enough. Katrinna had appeared from the bedroom (thin frame, five-foot-two and of halter tops, jeans, sometimes sneakers but mostly brown leather boots and heavily buckled decorative belts) just as Hector had run out to the corner to make a phone call. Katrinna had taken the spot on his dead grandmother's sofa, smoke twirling to the ceiling from a cigarette. Jerry was in the kitchen fighting the seal on a bottle of whisky, finally slitting it with a knife while knocking a glass onto the floor as Hector Lake appeared at the back door emitting an aura of renewed energy as he breezed in from outside.

"You're not fucking going to believe this, Lowe!" he'd said.

And Jerry remembers he couldn't help but cringe at those words and had tossed back a shot of whisky straight from the bottle—yeow—he remembered that had seemed to make it better. And he had to admit then, as he does now, sitting behind Delgado's Pet Mart, that it's true that he had chosen some time ago to live this way, a life of uncertainty incompatible with any notions of planning or a future, but when would he get used to it? When was there, in fact, going to be something solid to believe in, a respectable goal to aim for? Not to mention the conspicuous and unrelenting consumption of whisky. Somewhere along the line he must have decided that reality and illusion are indistinquishable, that nothing is constant and as a result it doesn't really matter most of the time what one does or how one does it. But if he really believes this, then why the cringing? At anything? Besides, he's often been eerily convinced that he isn't living at all, but *being lived*, a somewhat spooky conviction that there is something else that keeps the whole mess going regardless of what the heck he did. And, what's more, everything and everybody, even the Hector Moses Lakes of the world, are part of it. So why fear those words? Why fear anything?

Katrinna had called to Hector from the sofa, "Did you talk to The Man?"

Hector Lake passing through the kitchen—Oh, yeah, he'd talked to The Man.

Jerry Lowe had stayed put in the kitchen, hearing the two of them mumbling in the other room. Outside, two cats went at it, spitting and growling under the porch. Up the alley a horn honked, then honked again. Katrinna's voice heard rising, then Hector Lake's, snippets of conversation, and not wishing to hear any of it but unavoidable, as Hector Lake is heard calmly venting a description, although one can't quite be sure, of the stealing of a baby, some baby, all white.

Jesus Christ.

He begins to sweep up the broken glass, hopes he's drunk, his hearing impaired. Things are already getting out of hand and it's not even noon. Granny always said, *Be good young man*. And now one spends one's days sprawled on her dead sofa, being bad. Roll over, Granny, roll over in your grave. Don't see this. Turn those old sad eyes away and forgive your evil snake grandson. But there had still been a chance he hadn't heard right, sweeping the glass into a corner, gulping more whisky, grasping at straws. Sound trouble may only be temporary. And Hector Lake and Katrinna Reticuli were dope crazy at the best of times. There was a time in history, he's read, when they used to put all the crazies on boats and put them out to sea. *Narrenschiffs* they were called, literally Ships of Fools, great leaky ships full of crazies, the sea savage with currents and storms, the ships plunging, gouging, until they beached on some other unfortunate shore and dumped their unwanted load on someone else. Not a bad idea when you really thought about it.

The faded floral pattern of the carpet is discernible under his feet when he finally returns to the gloom of the living room. The curtains are still drawn. Groping for a chair, he notices a forgotten plant dying on the windowsill as he sits down. The room seems to roll, like, funny enough, a ship at sea. Clouds visible outside the window and it may just rain at some point. Maybe they were in for a blow. He is suddenly sensitive to details.

Hector Lake is ranting from the middle of the room.

"And The Man says on this he'll cop three bundles. That's nine hundred an' fifty beans worth right fucking there, man."

Jerry Lowe is back on his feet.

"You guys fucking crazy? Steal a fucking baby? A fucking baby for three fucking bundles? Jesus, fucking, shit, christ."

"You finished?" says Hector Lake. He has a pained expression. "Not a fucking kid, you dork. A cockatoo!"

And Jerry's mind did at that moment, he thinks quite appropriately now while sitting behind Delgado's Pet Mart, take flight. A cockatoo. Three bundles of the heroin drug for a cockatoo, a cockatoo baby birdie, all white. Oh, winged things in your heaven, and this, he had gulped without the whisky, would be what they would risk it all for that day.

Katrinna Reticuli's expression, on the other hand, was more akin to one of pity.

"Did you really think we were going to steal a kid, Jer?"

He'd regrouped. "Of course not."

But who'd cared what Katrinna thought. It was still crazy. And he sees again Hector Lake with thick arms raised, fingers nearly touching the water stain on the ceiling that looks to Jerry Lowe like an old man with a water bucket climbing a mountain. Hector towers, his muscles bulge. "These babies are worth twelve hundred—thirteen hundred bucks, man!"

"Thirteen hundred!"

"Fucking-A!"

"*Fucking-A, thirteen hundred . . .*" this he remembers mumbling while stepping around Hector and passing once more over the faded floral pattern on his way back to the kitchen. O, dope fiends in your early graves, did you hear that? Three bundles for a cockatoo. Seventy-five caps of the heroin drug in exchange for a birdie still pooping in its swaddling drawers. For anyone in the world to so want this particular type of baby. And enough to plunk thirteen hundred big ones on it!

None of this had seemed surprising to Hector.

"Believe it, Mr. Lowe," he'd continued. "There's big money in pets. Exotic ones anyway. Used to cop tropical fish from the pet store for my older brother in California. You know those weird-shaped guys with all the colours? Some of those little bastards ran four, five hundred. EACH."

And then having to grapple with another problem in his mind's eye—Hector Lake in a pet store, a conspicuous extra-large teenager approaching a tank of tropical fish—how in—

"You put a plastic bag full of water down your pants and just drop 'em in," explained Hector answering the unsaid question.

And, of course, he'd thought, these felonious simplistics. Anyone should know these things. And what's more, with all his experience, Hector Moses Lake would know. Hector Moses Lake would know how to steal a cockatoo. There had been a sickly sweet smell coming through an open window, more details. Flowers, he had become aware, flowers of some sort growing beneath the window. First time he'd noticed. The alley runs below, not fit for life, but something was growing there anyway.

Katrinna had dug out the dictionary.

"'Cockatoo; crested parrot'."

Hector Lake had smiled, the collective description of learned men apparently congruent with his own. "Right. It's like a parrot, only bigger. And has those big fucking feathers stickin' out of its head."

"Its plume," says Katrinna.

"Yeah. Its plume," says Hector Lake.

"Right. The plume," Jerry Lowe had echoed.

The plan then had been simple enough, Katrinna setting it down. She would be the duck, the decoy. Hector would grab the actual bird. And Jerry Lowe, thankful to be numbed with whisky, would, of course, be the driver.

Seeing the look on his face Katrinna had come to him, leaning down to his ear. "If thou remember'st not the slightest folly, that ever love did make thee run into, thou hast not loved . . ."

And Jerry had crossed the faded floral pattern a fourth time heading for the kitchen and more whisky—Ye scribes in fucknut heaven—Katrinna was no dummy—and where the heck did she get that one?

Then, in what seems only moments ago, Hector Lake was hunched beside him in the passenger seat of the shitbox with Katrinna in back, Hector Lake more nervous than he'd been back at the house possibly having realized that some things were more fun to just think about than actually go out and do. Jerry's mind was racing, in love and fear at the wheel, mickey of whisky cradled between his legs, in love possibly with Katrinna Reticuli, in fear of angry cons and over-crowded cell blocks when eventually busted for the heist. Our own little land-locked *Narrenschiff*, he'd thought, off on one's nutty deed. Give me your deranged, the emotionally warped. If Granny had left behind a rocker one could now be said to be off it, heading out through the lowlands and marshes to the Delta south of the city. And where somewhere on a wall sits a baby cockatoo worth three bundles of the heroin drug, over a thousand bucks' worth of tiny bones and feathers. He can almost see it sitting there on its perch in the local pet shop, dreaming cockatoo dreams, thinking cockatoo thoughts.

A small shopping plaza had appeared on the left and Hector Lake leaned forward.

"That's it. Go through the parking lot around back."

And Jerry had obeyed, guiding the shitbox around to the loading area behind the stores, not happy with what he first saw then and can still see now. Do Not Enter. No Parking. Authorized Vehicles Only.

"Don't worry about it," Hector had said, pointing out the target, until now a secret, and Jerry Lowe had backed the shitbox in near two red fire door exits. The sign above read: Delgado's Pet Mart.

A tan Lincoln Continental cruised slowly by, a moustached face grinning from the window.

"There's The Man," said Hector Lake. "What the fuck is he doing here? Asshole thinks it's hilarious. Back in a minute."

He pulled himself free of the shitbox and disappeared around the corner following the Lincoln.

"It is kind of funny," mused Katrinna. "Hector Lake stealing a bird."

"It's fucking nuts," said Jerry.

"Well, what do you suggest? We're sick, we're broke. Look, if he can get fish, he can get a bird."

And, you know, that almost made sense, he'd thought. And, of course, there's always Katrinna Reticuli herself. Katrinna Reticuli, who at the age of fifteen found herself locked up as a runaway by the nuns in Montreal. Who then escaped, married, and ended up pounding her husband within an inch of his life for ogling a girlfriend at a party, punching him out in the bathtub. Katrinna Reticuli who then lammed it to San Francisco and eventually north to Vancouver, fleeing a warrant for possession and prostitution. And the same Katrinna Reticuli who can quote Shakespeare and survived a two-year stint in the joint. She's not exactly new at this stuff either, he's forced to admit. She must know who can or can't do what.

Hector Lake then reappears from around the corner, leaning in the window to Katrinna.

"Okay. Got the layout. The bird's supposed to be on the left-hand wall when you go in. Shouldn't be too hard. There's only one guy in there."

"Okay. Give me a few minutes."

Katrinna squeezes out and is gone without so much as a by-your-leave, Jerry Lowe watching her go and any reassurance with her.

"She know what to do?"

"Are you kidding—" Hector Lake's head thrusts itself right into the car, his eyes drilling holes into those of Jerry Lowe. "—She's just got to keep that guy in there busy and it's a piece of cake. That's the hard part. But don't worry about Katrinna. And my part's easy—" the face of Hector Lake comes even closer "—and so's yours. Now tell me one thing you're not going to do."

Jerry Lowe is caught off-guard, his mind compiling a running list of possible no-no's.

"Bugger off?"

Hector Lake shuts his eyes, opens them again.

"You think I'd think you'd do that? Just whatever happens, keep this shitbox running. Right?"

"Right."

"I don't want to be pushing the fucker out of here."

"Okay, okay."

"I've done tougher jobs . . ."

"Uh huh."

". . . with the bozos sitting downstairs in their own house watching TV!"

"Right."

"Okay. I'll be coming out these doors in back right here, an' for fuck's sake, no matter what, no matter how long I am—" and their voices had joined in chorus "—*keep this shitbox running.*"

The head of Hector Lake had withdrawn, he remembers, then shoved itself in again.

"You know, we need this bird, Jerry, and I'm gonna get it no matter who or what may be stupid enough to get in the way," he'd said.

4

Big Birds

SO IT IS THAT JERRY LOWE finds himself sitting alone in back of Delgado's Pet Mart, those final words of Hector Lake still running through his mind. He feels he's in a movie, it isn't real. He's following a script written by someone else, he's doing his part and it's all in fun. In the movies at times like this some complication will usually arise to heighten the suspense. And this thought no sooner pops into his head than a semi-trailer backs in to the adjacent loading docks, blocking the path of the shitbox. He feels a rush of heat at the same time as his hands go cold. And the suspense, he notes, is indeed heightened. And one could even ask, staring out the windshield of the shitbox in disbelief, blasting away frantically on a cigarette, one could even ask, what is it with time anyway? When things are going well, it seems to run by like a retreating army. And then, for those other times, like now, it seems to take a seat on the pot to take a languid dump over a copy of the *Daily News*. And one can wonder some more while at it just how long is long while waiting for Hector Lake and Katrinna Reticuli, throwing nervous glances over one's shoulder at those back doors that Hector Lake is supposed to be, at some time, coming out of.

He fights his panic, this is no movie, brother. No stuntmen to stand in, a getaway assured by skilled professionals and clever editing. And those guys on the Safeway loading dock over there where the semi-trailer is parked are diddling the dog and that truck isn't ever going to move and he's trapped, a sitting duck behind Delgado's Pet Mart.

Confidence in Hector Lake and Katrinna Reticuli's abilities is waning. What's Hector doing in there? Sure, Hector can be tough, downright dangerous, but he can also be unpredictable, even charitable. One time he was surprised in a ground floor apartment he was ripping off, caught standing at the sliding door to the balcony with the guy's computer in his arms. The guy came in the front door and saw him and began crying, pleading with Hector not to do it, he was broke, he couldn't afford a new one, nothing was insured and he had child support payments and the list went on and on with Hector standing at the sliding door, one foot in and one foot out. Hector couldn't take it and put the computer back, asking only for fifty bucks cash (he got thirty-eight) and a jacket from the guy's closet that he'd liked.

His time for worrying is cut short as Hector Lake miraculously appears from out the back red fire doors of Delgado's Pet Mart, erect and moving towards the rust-primered shitbox. While the doors are open, a dog can be heard barking from somewhere inside the store along with assorted shrieks and wails of what he can only assume are other animals. Hector Lake is struggling with a huge cage that contains a flapping blur of white. Blood-curdling squawks and shrieks emanate from the white blur as Jerry shifts around, flinging the passenger door open and fighting an immediate impulse to flee, to get the fuck out of there. He does manage a piece of panic-driven advice to Hector Lake who thunders on, fighting with the bird cage.

"It ain't gonna fucking fit, man!"

"It'll fit!" and somehow the cage is bent, mashed, bashed, and beaten into the space behind the passenger seat of the rust-primered shitbox. Then Hector Lake mashes himself into the front seat, barking out a single word: "Drive!"

Jerry Lowe looks ahead—praise the script writers—and the semi-truck has disappeared, gone in the confusion of the last minutes. He pulls out of the loading area, no time to look for pursuit or attending to the frenzied white blur going ape-shit in the back seat and it strikes him a reassuring thought that anything this ludicrous could never be criminal. He turns onto the main road where Hector Lake directs him a block south and into a restaurant parking lot. Hector Lake is fidgeting around with his hand and looking serious.

"All right. Go back and get the duck!"

Jerry Lowe swallows. One fucking bird was the deal.

"*Katrinna*, you asshole!" shouts Hector Lake, doing something to his finger.

Jerry Lowe, grabbing for door handles, hurries out onto the road to collect Katrinna, Katrinna spotted there up the road a bit, sauntering along—jesus christ, just out for an easy stroll. *Get a move on, Katrinna, for god's sake.*

Back at the shitbox, the cage's mangle of wire mesh, Jerry Lowe is aware, is visible to the world through the back window. He climbs in, backs the shitbox out of the parking lot and gets it headed back along the main road. Katrinna is the first to speak.

"This bird all right?"

Hector Lake's head snaps around and the pointing finger of his right hand can now be seen to be wrapped in the bloody pages thirty and thirty-one of *Fat City* by Leonard Gardiner.

"That fucker's lucky to be alive! I swear the son of a bitch KNEW he was being stolen for christ's sake. Fucker bit me. I didn't know those fuckers bite!"

Katrinna's voice changes tone.

"I don't know much about birds, let alone cockatoos, but this guy looks pretty big to be a baby . . ."

Hector Lake doesn't like it.

"You telling me—I went to the wall The Man said. It was the only white cockatoo I freaking saw—the only white BIRD I freaking saw!"

"Just curious."

"Well, fine time to think about that. Christ!"

All three now fall silent. The bird is still squawking in a frenzy and clawing at its cage, Jerry Lowe keeping a nervous eye on the rearview mirror and Hector Lake is right. This is not the fucking time to start wondering. About anything. Of this they can all be sure, Hector Moses the surest of all.

"No way," he keeps repeating. "No freaking way . . ."

He unwraps pages thirty and thirty-one of *Fat City* from his finger and re-dresses it in pages thirty-four and thirty-five. Jerry Lowe drives on, denying himself the hazards of reflection but still asking the one big question: "Three bundles for a cockatoo?"

5

Fuzzballs

OFFICER SYLVAIN DEACON PEERS OUT through the windshield of the squad car at the house at 157 Victoria Drive. From the front yard two huge mangy wolfhounds eyeball him through a dilapidated fence from a bashed and beaten, now mostly mud, one-time lawn. From the house can be heard shouts and the occasional sound of things smashing.

"It's ten-thirty in the morning," says his partner, Styler Ferguson. "What are these assholes doing?"

"Welfare day, old sport," replies Sylvain Deacon.

Styler Ferguson drawls into the mike. "Six-fourteen, Ferguson, one-five-seven Victoria Drive. Domestic. Mayday. Mayday. We're going in."

Sylvain Deacon opens the driver's side door. "Keep laughing, Ferg. Only one more day of this for me."

And that much was true, his long lean body, six-feet-four-and-a-half inches of it, now stretching itself outside the car. One more day and he was out of there. Three week's vacation time with no more citations. No more drunks, pimps, hypes and other fuzzballs. No more grunge coffee. Just three well-deserved weeks of chi-chis sipped by the pool with Mrs. Deacon soaking up the sun by his side. Three weeks of restaurant dining, room service, maybe motor scooters whirring out along a tropical coast road to some private spot sheltered by a broad-leafed marquee.

"Hey, Deac. Wait up."

Sylvain Deacon finds himself standing at the front gate staring at the hounds. Styler Ferguson approaches the fence, putting on his hat. "Better wait for me, pal. Don't know what these bozos are going to do." He looks up at the house. "What a racket. Lot of demolition going on in there. Domestic bliss. I see crap like this and I think, don't ever get married, Fergy, boy. Don't ever get married. Then again, I see you and Lucille, what, twelve years? And I think, shit, maybe I *should* get married."

Sylvain Deacon looks down at his younger, shorter partner.

Yes, Ferg. So maybe you should. Best thing to ever do for some. But find a woman like Lucille first, which won't be easy. One has to have someone for this job. Someone detached, but there. Someone kept at a distance but who cares, so there's somewhere to spill your guts now and then when things get rough. Like when that doped-up kid fired on you those three months back and you went down, not from a bullet but from the fear. That bullet it did come close, Ferg. And you shit your pants. Who wouldn't. That's the worst of it. A bullet in the guts or shit in your pants. Those are the choices. But for me, Ferg, I went home that night and talked to Lucille. She made dinner and sat. And she'd take shit in her pants anytime she said, over a hole in the head. And you went out and got plastered and talked to the boys, anyone who would listen. And that's the other way to do it, Ferg. That's the other way.

The two hounds have commenced howling from the other side of the fence. There are mounds of dog shit everywhere. From behind the screen door up the sagging front steps of the house a woman's voice bellows something unintelligible above the commotion. Styler Ferguson tenses and leans over.

"Think these mothers bite?"

Sylvain Deacon lifts his hat, runs his hand through silver hair.

"The dogs or the people inside?"

He straightens, hooking his thumbs into his belt and calls up to the door. At the sound of his voice the hounds go really crazy, howling louder. Two sets of watery blood-shot eyes widen through the fence. Styler Ferguson steps back a few paces, feeling for the butt of his revolver. The screen door comes open with a screech on its hinges, thrown back by a thick bare arm quivering with the lurid colours of a tattoo. A woman appears looking hostile, her breasts unrestricted and tugging against the almost transparent confines of a tattered wine-stained T-shirt.

"SHUT THE FUCK UP, YOU!"

Styler Ferguson stiffens—good christ, does she mean them or the dogs?

The dogs act like a switch has been thrown, their heads ducking low and tongues dragging through the mud and shit as they silently skulk to the side of the house. Sylvain Deacon speaks calmly.

"We've received a complaint—"

"YEAH? FROM WHO?"

The muffled voice of a man comes faintly from inside the house. The woman turns, issuing the same command she's just given the dogs. The muffled voice falls silent.

Sylvain Deacon opens the gate, advances part way up the wobbly front steps. Styler Ferguson follows a few steps behind, his eyes on where the hounds have just gone and the many mounds of dog shit.

"We've received a complaint, ma'am, that there's been some trouble . . . "

"TROUBLE?"

Styler Ferguson is sure her breasts separate, then come together with a clap.

"WHAT TROUBLE? WHO CALLED?"

Sylvain Deacon has stopped two steps down from the porch, his eyes now at the same level as the straining wine-stained T-shirt, his long lean body listing with the stairs. Odour of cigarettes, alcohol, and dog shit in the air. A bird chirps from somewhere out back and the tattoo on the fleshy arm is now visible, a writhing serpent coiled around an equally writhing naked woman with the words: Die Trying.

The hand of Styler Ferguson once again feels for the butt of his revolver, his eyes darting back and forth between the woman and where the hounds have gone, unsure as to which is the most dangerous. A man, hairless and with a belly like a balloon, appears phantom-like in the doorway.

"WHAT'S GOING ON?"

The woman turns.

"YOU STAY THE FUCK OUTTA THIS."

No one speaks for a moment and Sylvain Deacon thinks he feels a few drops of rain but the sky's clear. The woman turns back to Sylvain Deacon.

"We had a little argument, but it's over now."

"FUCK YOU IT IS," says Bald and Bellied.

The woman turns back.

"LOOK YOU FUCKER. I SAID I WOULD AN' I WILL."

"MY ASS YOU WILL."

"YOUR ASS?"

"MY ASS."

"OKAY!"

Now the woman is in full steam down the steps, knocking Sylvain Deacon aside. Styler Ferguson leaps to safety, with but inches to spare dodging the dog shit, the woman marching to the back of the house and stomping barefoot through the mud and setting the hounds to howling again. Sylvain Deacon manages to hold Bald and Bellied, who tries to follow and calls after her, "YOU'RE FUCKING CRAZY LUCILLE. YOU KNOW THAT?"

"Lucille?" says Styler Ferguson.

Sylvain Deacon gives him a threatening look.

"Go see what she's doing."

Styler Ferguson hesitates. From back of the house comes the sound of something being scraped. Then a thumping and scratching from somewhere above and Styler Ferguson moves reluctantly to the side of the house. A grunt from overhead and Styler Ferguson looks up and calls his partner. Sylvain Deacon moves down the steps, Bald and Bellied following. Sylvain shields his eyes to squint up to where Styler Ferguson is now pointing. Silhouetted against the sun and straddling the rooftop stands a naked shadowy figure that moments ago stood at the front screen door, clothed at least. Sylvain Deacon squints harder, rewarded with the discovery of another tattoo that is now visible on the shadowy inside of a naked thigh—good jesus—down *there*. Bald and Bellied stands wheezing beside him, finally compelled to say something by the ugly turn things have taken.

"Been sayin' she'll jump off the roof if I don't admit to screwing her sister. I never screwed her sister!"

A crowd of neighbours have now gathered about the front gate. The shoulders of Sylvain Deacon appear to sag, taking on an unseen burden as Styler Ferguson hunches at his side.

"What we do now, boss?"

Bald and Bellied moves off to the side, looking a little more confident having now the visible proof of his earlier diagnosis of the lady Lucille.

"You see? I told you she was crazy!"

Sylvain Deacon remains motionless staring up at the rooftop, not the most intelligent thing to do at a time like this. Gives the mind too much time to think. And ask questions. Like, how does it happen, all this? Twenty or so years of treading the obnoxious leavings of other's lives, hoping to what? Make a difference? Make the world a better place? This kind of reflection while on one's own time may be normal, but when it starts happening while on the job it's a sign of getting old, burning out. How hard to imagine you were ever anybody else, like a kid for instance, who's watched geese honking across a prairie sky while your dad comes out on the front porch to say he smells a good rain coming.

He notices the naked figure above has now moved to the end of the roof, no longer blocking the sun and leaving it free to move on. Even the birds heard earlier seem to have fled, Nature knows when to take a powder. And the rooftop figure is now pointing down to, and explaining what may in a moment be, her final goddamned resting place if Bald and Bellied doesn't own up. One of the hounds trots over as if in compliance and drops a steamer on the exact spot. Styler Ferguson mumbles something about calling the fire department.

Sylvain Deacon gathers himself.

"It's okay, Ferg. I'll handle it. And there's enough dog shit piled up around here to break anyone's fall."

Then to Bald and Bellied: "Did you screw her sister?"

"WHAT? ARE YOU NUTS?"

"Well, tell her you did."

"WHAT?"

Sylvain Deacon's voice is low and even.

"Well, sir, I sure as hell didn't, but right now you two are screwing me, so tell her."

"YOU GOTTA BE KIDDIN' ME."

"Are those your dogs?"

"YEAH, BUT—"

"Well, tell your friend up there you screwed her sister or I'm gonna shoot your dogs and then I'm gonna shoot YOU."

"WHAT?"

Sylvain Deacon pulls his pistol. Bald and Bellied backs away, throwing a questioning glance at Styler Ferguson. Can this be happening, what is this? This cop is nuts. His eyes have glazed over, like raku pots. He's zombied out, he should be retired. What in God's name does this asshole think he's doing?

Sylvain Deacon is striding to the side of the house. Styler Ferguson throws him a questioning glance of his own and begins to follow. The hounds are in a frenzy, like they know what may be coming. With frightened bulging eyes they watch the coming of Sylvain Deacon. Bald and Bellied wrings his hands, looking up and down the street for some kind of assistance. Finally he raises his eyes to the roof.

"AWRIGHT! I SCREWED YOUR SISTER!"

Sylvain Deacon stops walking. The hounds howling is replaced with some milder whining. From the rooftop comes nothing, then a soul-piercing shriek. From the crowd at the front gate there comes a triumphant roar as the figure on the rooftop turns to descend, and there's no doubt in anyone's mind who she's coming for.

Bald and Bellied is sprinting up the front steps and into the house. Appearing again at full speed, he takes the steps down two at a time and squeezes through the front gate, cheered on by the crowd of supporters gathered there, a case of beer and a pair of shoes clutched in his arms. And calling back in a last sense of fair play: "PLEASE DON'T TAKE IT OUT ON THE DOGS, LUCILLE."

By the side of the house Styler Ferguson has moved forward, duty calling, taking gently the gun from the hand of his partner. Back in the car, the radio unit crackles relaying messages. One to keep watch for a man in his late forties believed armed in a stolen red Honda two-door, licence number PGN-801. And the other for any vehicle carrying an adult white cockatoo with no legal proof of purchase.

6

Six-armed Statuettes

SHADOWS DANCE OVER THE LANE from laundry hung along the backyard lines. An immense pair of coveralls hanging in one yard makes whapping noises in the breeze. Beneath the laundry a grid-work of neighbourhood fences run and a dog barks somewhere. A garden gate slams and a kid lets out a wail from down the block.

The two of them stand in a white stuccoed garage looking down on a shape that can just be made out in the shadows. The shape groans a little from where it lies on the garage floor. Slivers of light stray in from a cracked window that at one time was painted over as one speaks to the other, his voice hushed and urgent.

"Come on, man . . ."

"That should teach him. *Kutta*."

"Come on, Singh. You wanna kill him?"

"White fucker fucks with my sister."

"Yeah, well, fucker this and fucker that. Let's go, man."

The one takes the other by the arm and pulls him out to the car. They climb in, Singh Sidhu behind the wheel, Jagit Sanghera in the other side. The Camaro gleams in the sunlight, metallic green. Its hind-end is jacked high in the air and hangs suspended over two huge rear tires. Jagit calls the Camaro the Green Behemoth. From between the rear wheels two mouths of chrome poke out from down under. The chrome catches the sunlight as Singh Sidhu guns the engine. The chrome mouths roar, the roar subsiding to a steady rumble that pervades the entire car. They rumble slowly up the alley. Where the alleyway meets the street Singh guns it again. The rear tires spin, spewing gravel and then letting out a shriek as the rubber contacts the pavement.

"Yeah, man!" lets go Jagit Sanghera, whapping the dashboard bongo style. Flips a CD into the player and cranks the volume, the four coaxial speakers erupting as music booms from window to window. Singh Sidhu shouts above the noise, still steamed.

"Should maybe kill that mother!"

A small bird swoops down and narrowly misses being beaned on the windshield.

"Look out bird," shouts Jagit Sanghera. "Save yo' ass!"

Singh Sidhu is still contemplating the problem of the white guy and his sister.

"Look, man," says Jagit Sanghera. "So he likes your sister. Your sister likes him. Big deal. With your old man around what could ever come of it?"

"His you-know-what up her you-know-where. That's what!"

"For fuck's sake, man."

"Shit, she's dumb sometimes. Can you see the old man if she brought a white guy home?"

Jagit Sanghera beats a rhythm to the music.

"Well, there you go. Your old man would never allow it. The old school. That's your old man. An' you should know that at least."

They stop at a light, Singh Sidhu reaching over to turn down the music.

"Right about that, fuckhead."

Jagit Sanghera grins, faking a cower against the door. From the mirror two pink fuzzballs swing crazily.

"Sorry, man."

"Hardly fucking funny."

"Shashi's not that bad, man."

"Shashi-Gashy."

"No, really. She's okay, man."

"You marry her then."

"Not me, man. It's your old man, man, and his ways. Not mine."

"My old man and his ways."

"Your old man's okay, man."

"Get him drunk and hit him with a hammer, man."

"Oh, man, man."

Jagit turns up the volume again and they drive a few blocks not speaking. They cruise up Kingsway, pulling into a Brownie's Chicken.

"You go," says Singh, handing Jagit some money.

Singh stays in the car, watches Jagit saunter wise-ass across the lot. A slightly crazy bugger, that Jagit, he thinks. Claims he can still remember when his older brother was brought into the house off the streets of Kanpur, Jagit five-and-a-half years old as his mother freaked out, his brother's body laid out on the table. Some kind of street fight and the colour red Jagit had just learned meant luck to the Chinese, but the red on his brother's shirt had meant something else to his mother, who fell down at one point and had to be helped up. His old man was away, in Canada, and money and papers had come only the week before that Jagit had watched his mother get all happy about and he'd wished then with his brother laid out on the table that that money and those papers could have come again getting her back to that state. And Jagit can still remember washing the rice, he says, the old lady saying: "Three times Jagit. Once for the ancestors. Twice for the guests. And a third time for the Gods."

Singh Sidhu himself can vaguely recall a crush of people, the air heavy with noise, heat and dust, the braying of a goat, while down along the river adults splashed prayers and bathed in the fast-flowing muddy water. Another country, four years old himself when they left. And not any real allegiance for him there, not like the folks had.

Jagit Sanghera is leering out through the window of Brownie's, waiting for the order. Singh Sidhu leers back. Jagit Sanghera can afford to fool around, his life was simple. His parents didn't put too much stock in the old traditional ways, at least not where their kids were concerned.

He lights a cigarette, gripped again with The Fear. A cloud of smoke billows in the front seat and curls a fuliginous serpent over the steering wheel. Everything gets a bit hazy, like being viewed from behind a fine sheet of gauze. His head feels light and he seems to be shrinking. A crow out of nowhere swoops down and does a quick dance on the hood of the car, a big shiny black thing that aims an evil looking black eye at him through the windshield. He honks the horn to scare it off as Jagit Sanghera appears through the gauze, coming across the lot clutching two bags. Singh Sidhu watches the smoke now curling up and along the roof of the car, the same smoke into which, he thinks, the lives of all young men forced to follow old country traditions are likely to go up in.

And then there's what he's come to know as The Fear. It hadn't really taken hold until a bright morning, outside, a few weeks ago. The grass was still wet with dew, he remembers, and birds were yammering in the trees. His father had come outside and stood looking at him from the front steps.

"Singh," his father had said. "Shashi Bhattal."

Singh was working on the Green Behemoth and had thought: What? Is that a city, father? A rock band?

"One's wife to be," his father had said. "Her father and I have agreed. It's a good match."

He'd fumbled then with a spark plug asking himself hopeless silent questions. Oh, and where was your son Singh Sidhu through all this? WHO is your son Singh Sidhu? Are these the old ways again, father?

"These are the ways, the best ways. I'm very pleased. It's a weight off my mind, Singh."

And he was unable to find the words, might have said, Ack, Ack, or something like that. Then had said something stupid—"She's the fat one isn't she?"—the old man coming down from the steps hand raised and then descending, like a family tree, across a cheek. Had caused his eyes to roll, he remembered, just like it says in books.

"Don't disgrace me."

"Sorry, father."

"She is healthy. Good. You want children?"

I have a choice, father? (This thankfully was not said).

"It worked well for your mother and I," his father continued, "The old way. We had never met when we were married. All Delhi rejoiced. The Ganges ran pink with blossoms, cattle formed a sacred procession and moved out of our way when we walked. Holy men offered us their bowls and the clouds of incense could be seen all the way to Rangoon!"

His father, like himself, had a vivid imagination. This was bullshit, of course. Pop was losing it, he'd known this for months. Pop worked too hard, worried constantly about the erosion of traditions, the break-down of Indian beliefs in the community, the violence that appeared prevalent in a lot of the Asian guys his age. Singh had wiped his hands madly with a rag at this point and pretended to be really busy now, looking under the hood of the Green Behemoth as his stomach tied in knots. Sure, sure, Pop. And you have reaped two fine children. And I am the body of one and my sister the body of another, a white-guy-loving daughter, and I, your non-traditional son.

"Shashi likes you, my son."

This is unlikely.

"She is healthy and good."

She is big, father, and strange.

"One day, grandchildren . . ."

And he'd stared dumbly down the driveway, unable to meet his father's eyes.

His stomach knots again with the memory, the half-eaten chicken and milkshake not sitting well there in the Green Behemoth parked in the Brownie's parking lot. His hands hang suddenly like dread over the steering wheel, a wad of coleslaw dropped and seeping through his pantleg.

He'd had a dream. Some kind of sexual laison with Shashi Bhattal with clouds of incense billowing up from a six-armed god statuette on a rickety bedside table, the activity in the bed, never clearly envisioned, causing the table to topple and a terrible fire after.

He drops the rest of his chicken and shake out the window.

The folks have always said he has a heck of an imagination, but boy. If they only knew the half of it. The old man doesn't know dick. Shashi Bhattal is dangerous, nuts, all our women are. And he sure as heck must not have heard of Phoolan Devi, the bandit queen from Central India, Pop, the central part of one's own country. All of twenty-two when she finally gave herself up to the cops, wanted at the time for armed robbery, kidnapping and seventy or so murders. And who cares if it's true. A warning is a warning. Blitzed twenty men in the village of Behmai alone, Papa, believing that village was hiding the guy who killed her lover, so they say. And maybe the poor bastards were. One has seen the newspaper photograph, father, this lady isn't even ugly, good-looking, in fact, and (get this, man), "considered very intelligent and respectful of her people." Before she went nuts, that is. Yes, Pop, there's bad stuff on the horizon with this Shashi Bhattal thing. Her brother has confided that when she rages she can turn a guy's balls to jelly, blood to *balgam*. Life to shit, father, the times they are a-changing you dumb old fart and come this night your son, the good Singh Sidhu, is going to get pissed, believe it, oh, yes. You'll have yourself one asshole *nashebaz* to deal with this night.

It isn't until twenty minutes later, when crossing the Cambie Bridge with a vague plan to meet up with Jagit's younger brother downtown, that Jagit Sanghera asks, "You okay, Singh?"

"Yeah, I'm okay," says Singh.

"You sure?"

"Yeah, I'm sure."

"WELL SLOW FUCKING DOWN THEN, MAN."

Singh Sidhu glances at the speedometer and eases up on the gas pedal.

"Look, Singh, can we just forget this Shashi thing and your old man. Alright?"

Jagit implores him with a look. Singh Sidhu nods, their eyes meeting for a moment, just enough time for the fuse to burn down, as both of them erupt with laughter. And be it a tenuous shared insight into some absurdity or whatever, possibly the affinity of the world of the Ganges honking its muddy brown waters into the sea and draining off the humble muck and prayers of millions from the northern badlands of their birthplace, a murky jugular choked with famine and spit, as here, not much is that different with the Fraser River to the south opening its own muddy maw into the Gulf and carrying the beer cans, auto parts, condoms and prayers of the white guys onto the beaches, the sand no longer golden but battleship grey and signs posted: Closed For Swimming. It was, really, when you came right down to it, just too freaking crazy all 'round to get too bent out of shape about.

A short time later he watches as Jagit Sanghera leans a thigh against the pool table under the dim lights of the beer parlour. Both are awaiting the shot of Jagit's younger brother, the brother younger pointing with his cue what ball's going to go where.

Twelve in the side.

"No fucking way," says Jagit Sanghera.

A click as the balls connect. From where he's sitting Singh Sidhu can see the tops of the balls flashing just above the rail of the pool table. A thunk as the twelve ball finds the side pocket. Jagit Sanghera says something and the body of the brother younger can be seen once again upright, moving around the table.

And the pool game, at least, is proceeding as it should, thinks Singh Sidhu. Any decent game is always carried out with a minimum of movement and theatrics and verbal exchanges, the latter preferably never being of more than two- to three-word sentences.

Where-to?

Combo, three-corner. One-bank-side.

It's a comfort, something predictable and at the same time the outcome unpredictable. But safe, after all, it's only a game. And true, there are rules. And even traditions. And, true again, you had to respect them. But the choice of whether to play or not was there, at least. He can't be rid of The Fear. It disappears for short periods but always surfaces again. The planned marriage to Shashi Bhattal was making him nutty, an overwhelming feeling of desperation was beginning to tarnish everything. He suddenly remembers some past and believed forgotten highschool biology lesson: ". . . the female spider is particularily venomous and it's still believed by some that a man, once bitten, experiences great pain, then dances, then dies."

He can't remember what kind of spider, but it was the female. He pushes some quarters across the table to Jagit who's about to sit down.

"Put on some music."

"On this jukebox?" says Jagit.

"Why not?"

Jagit scoops the coins.

"Okay, pawtnaw."

Singh Sidhu sits back. Yeah, so what. There's something to be said for that cowboy stuff when you're not feeling shit-hot. Could get a hat, some boots, learn to roll cigarettes one-handed and then drive the pickup into the sunset and love only a good horse.

The brother younger is preparing for another shot. He runs the cue back and forth, getting the angle. A difficult hook-shot on the eight-ball; the ball, Singh Sidhu notices, from the brother younger's position anyway, Singh's sitting directly behind.

7

Bugga-Bugga

HECTOR LAKE, AS A YOUNG AND TALENTED high school quarterback in Santa Barbara, begins what would become a major transformation after viewing the face of young Virginia through the hospital glass, that mask of scars and bitterness voicing through the pain that it does not wish to see his somewhat damaged face again, ever, and he avoids her parents by leaving by the hospital service stairs out back as soon as he is physically able. He himself sustains only a minor cut to his head and a fractured left ankle, hobbling down the back lane between the service vehicles in a fresh and still-wet walking cast and wondering why he was left able to do this while Virginia, lying scarred and smashed three floors above and unable to move, no longer The Woman of Great Beauty but forever changed, is made to suffer more and longer, the plastic surgery alone going on for years.

The following months brandish spears of guilt on a daily basis at his young conscience, jabbing and sometimes drawing blood as he attempts to parry them in a continual binge of pills and alcohol. But it's not all pain-related, this onset of wildness and addiction, in the beginning it's just more fun to get high than not. The lime-green Toyota used for delivering pizzas is laid to rest one hot summer's night in a four-wheel skid at the corner of Turner and Burke, its whole right side caved in against the seats from the impact of the other car, Hector somehow again escaping a crash unscathed, having fallen forward under the dash at the point of impact, his head crammed against the passenger side floor vent as warm and traumatized pizzas ooze three different types of cheese from the quashed back seat.

His father bears the brunt of his son's fall, answering for the family when called upon. *For god's sake, do something, Murray.*

Hector opens the door for his father who shuffles in, a logo for Mr. Lake's machine parts business visible on the left breast of his sports shirt. Mr. Lake takes a seat keeping silent on the mess the place is in.

"Your mother's very concerned . . ."

Hector nods out in the chair opposite, he's been trying something new, something that really does kill pain, really does make everything better, and a lit cigarette (he's begun smoking too) falls to the carpet from his fingers. Mr. Lake reaches for it and puts it out, leaves five twenties on the table and closes the door behind him.

Hector's two charges for driving under the influence loom greater and he hears of the warrants from his brother, the only one left in the family who will talk to him. There are also rumours of charges being laid by Virginia's family for his part in her accident.

"You could clean up, Hector. Do some time, maybe. Pay a fine. You'd get your license back in a year or so. What about that football scholarship to UCLA? Pay your dues and put it behind you. You could do that, Hector. The folks'll come around. It'll be okay."

"I got to be somewhere," says Hector.

He skips to San Francisco living off the odd B&E, hustling and then robbing gays in North Beach bars and selling drugs. He adapts well to the street, still having a good mind when not too high, planning his plays as he once did on the football field. But things close in and it hits him while racing through Golden Gate Park in a hurry to make a buy, that if he gets pulled up by the cops for anything, anything at all—like, jay-walking—he's screwed. The warrants would show and it'd be over, he'd be locked up for sure. Alternatives are few and there's nothing else to do but keep heading north, to Vancouver, Canada, maybe. He's heard it has a good drug scene and by this time that's all that really matters.

The first meeting of Hector Lake and Jerry Lowe takes place one Vancouver evening while Hector's running down Hastings Street after a drug deal gone wrong. The buyer had stabbed him twice and taken off up the street with the money and the drugs. Hector had given chase, the knife in one hand which the guy dropped upon taking off, and holding his stomach with his other. Hector is hoofing it in Reebok NFL Game Day black and white crosstrainers and is almost gaining on the guy, wound and all. He approaches the Blue Eagle Café just as Jerry is coming out having gone in to warn Katrinna and others that the narcotics cops are just outside watching the place from across the street. The narcotics cops are getting ready to pounce and come across the road just as the guy Hector Lake is chasing flies by. Hector Lake comes churning along the sidewalk, breathing heavily and clutching his side, a patch of blood visible through his sweatshirt. Four narcotics cops leap onto the sidewalk. Two continue on into the café to put choke holds on whoever they can. Through the window Jerry sees one grab Katrinna just as a third slams him up against the doorway. The fourth officer, dressed in blue jeans and a black leather jacket, heads Hector off as he tries to sprint by. He knows Hector, knows what and who he is, but when he sees the blood he makes the call for an ambulance. Hector leans against the doorway beside Jerry, sweating heavily and gripping his side.

"Guy ripped me off," he manages to gasp.

Jerry Lowe is impressed. This guy is something else, running down the street after being stabbed in the gut. And the guy's big, not fat big, but built big, pumped big. Unknown to Jerry Lowe at the time, but, as he rightly assumes, Hector Lake manages to stay in shape by continually getting arrested on minor beefs affording him six-month stints in the slammer where he can refuel on three squares a day and work out pumping iron in the weight pits. In this way Hector becomes, for a short time, an athlete of sorts again. In fact, if it wasn't for getting arrested and serving time every now and then, he would most likely waste away to a shadow like any other regular heroin user. As it is, he maintains a formidable size, an obvious asset for anyone doing business on the street.

On a hot afternoon a week after their Hastings Street meeting, the two of them walked through Chinatown.

Hector was out to score dope, Jerry was along for the ride. Jerry didn't do narcotics, only rarely did a drug deal. Katrinna was the user, he was the drinker. Hector Lake did whatever was handy.

The sidewalks teem with people, mostly Asian. Hector stopping to light a cigarette. Wafts of barbecued meat, braised fowl and things being steamed mingle with the smell of exhaust from the slow-moving cars along the street. In a window beside them glazed ducks hang in a row. Little vials of herbs and twisted root-type things are lined up along the sill. In a slightly larger jar an unidentifiable object stands on its end against the sides of the jar. TIGER TESTICLES—$25.00.

"Supposed to get you horny," Jerry says but Hector isn't listening. He's watching the crowd around him from behind his sunglasses.

"This is not a good place to be scoring, I'll tell you, Mr. Lowe," he says. "See these people? They're crazy, man. Look at 'em. It's a freaking zoo down here. You ever try to get through here in a hurry, Lowe? Forget it. Cops chased me once, right up here. The sidewalks were packed, like now, an' everyone doddlin' along. I felt like a fucking bowling ball. Was knockin' 'em left and right and they all screaming, 'Bugga-bugga! Bugga-bugga!' Or something like that. It was hopeless. When the cops finally caught me up at the corner there I looked back and all I could see were pissed-off faces for a block long and all looking the hate at me. I may be exaggerating now but I swear all their teeth were gnashing. That's how bad it was. It reminded me of when I split home, that's how all the people looked there. All the family, anyway. At least they did to me."

Jerry Lowe maintains his silence, respectful of Hector's ragged and gnawing memories as they move ahead through the crowd, Hector taking some extra care not to jostle anyone.

8

Sun, Moon and Earth

JERRY LOWE HAS ALWAYS SUSPECTED there is more to events than meets the eye. That is, there are connections, vast and untraceable. When something happens somewhere, some other event is likely to be triggered somewhere else as a not-too-obvious result. Or something. The Butterfly Effect.

He knows, for instance (just how, exactly, he doesn't know), that the moon is now in its *perigee*, that time when it comes closest to Earth, thus exerting its strongest influence. He also knows that the sun, moon, and Earth are at this time aligned, this phenomenon happening only once or twice a year and with a weird name all its own which he doesn't know. And the comet Encke (or is it Ritana?) is cruising closely by, spewing stardust and other shit into the cosmos. But while sitting at the wheel of the rust-primered shitbox and rolling back to the city from the Delta, the cockatoo still going nuts from the space behind the back seat and with Hector Lake and Katrinna Reticuli planning their next move, whatever images he has unconsciously ferreted from recent late-night TV news bulletins and absent-minded glances at newspapers found in restaurants, all these now come winging freely into his mind. There have been record high tides, record storms, record flooding. Everywhere there seems a climate and nature imbalance. And human-based disasters have their own headlines: trains careening off cliffs, planes blowing apart in the sky. And there also seems an unusually high number of the lonely and berserk running through shopping malls and fast-food joints blasting away with Uzis at anything that moves. Even schools aren't safe and kids killing kids is no longer news.

He allows his mind to spin its newsreel of the world's present chaos, possibly in an attempt to explain his own. What a time to steal a cockatoo. One should take more seriously one's morning horoscope. "A bad time to invest." "Romance and crime not favourable." And it seems not too far-fetched to believe that the earth could just open up, at any time, a huge fissure under your rolling arse and down into the big hungry yap of a world gone mad one goes.

"Ever wonder how anything survives at all?" he says out loud.

Hector Lake and Katrinna stop talking, only for a moment, they don't need any more weird shit right now. The bird is still going ape and Hector's finger hurts like hell, and at least Katrinna is doing something useful like figuring what to do with the dope when they finally get it.

"I think we should see Bobby. He'll turn some over. And we got to go to the doctor's. Before we go home."

They're passing the airport. The fence at the end of the runway banks along their left. A giant passenger jet lifts above them by what seems to Jerry Lowe a distance of only a few feet. His eardrums pound with the rush of jet engines. This isn't needed. No new disaster headlines wanted. He glances upward through the windshield, sees the belly of the plane, jesus, it *is* just inches. Stay up there you bastards sipping your martinis, thinking you'll live forever. Just don't crash now.

He feels a new wave of the old anxiety and notices all the whisky's gone. He slides the empty bottle under the seat. The bridge into town appears in the distance, just a lick and a split and they could be home. Safe. From crazy planets and falling planes, the something elses. But Hector Lake and Katrinna Reticuli have other plans, junkies always do. And why should his life be any different or more predictable than the lonely and berserk? He has, after all, chosen to live this way.

He pushes his foot down on the accelerator, the steely knob down in the shadows still with a piece of Hector Lake's leather hanging off it, but not much happens.

Far too many hours later Hector Lake and Katrinna Reticuli are chatting it up, treating the entire day like it's all been a Sunday drive, Hector Lake swigging from a freshly opened forty-ouncer of whisky Jerry Lowe moments ago picked up in a quick dash into the liquor store. It is, in fact, a Tuesday, not a Sunday, and Jerry Lowe feels that he and he alone is aware they're stuck in rush-hour downtown traffic with the cockatoo still throwing fits through the back window of the shitbox from its mashed-up cage behind the back seat. Upon coming off the bridge into town Hector and Katrinna had insisted on hitting the doctor's office for an interim hit of methadone, which they are entitled to, both being on a government-sponsored drug program for recovering heroin addicts, albeit they were not actually one hundred percent recovering. The meth would tide them over until the deal was done and the cockatoo was exchanged for the better stuff. This was not the best thing for Jerry Lowe, he'd seen the different effects of the meth and heroin. Minutes after taking meth, the subject would most often become someone else, more aggressive, louder and more obnoxious and more likely to make a fool of themselves in public. On the heroin everyone is better behaved, wanting only to sit somewhere and nod out, the biggest problem simply being to put out any fires caused by dropped and burning cigarette butts.

The doctor's clinic is downtown in the West End, and they'd arrived there, it seems to Jerry, a million years ago. Hector and Katrinna are out of the car and heading for the clinic doors almost before he gets the shitbox stopped. He gets out too and stands a moment in the parking lot leaning slightly to the left. The moon, he still knows, rolls somewhere in its perigee. And the cops, he knows, habitually roll by doctor's offices who are known to prescribe methadone for addicts, keeping an eye on things. The cockatoo, still thrashing in its cage and completely visible through the rear window of the shitbox, is like a beacon to anyone that something wasn't right with this picture.

He lights a cigarette and calls after Katrinna Reticuli and Hector Lake.

"So I just sit here?"

From the doorway to the clinic Katrinna Reticuli shoots him a glance, even looks a mite fearful at his tone of voice and says something to Hector Lake, who walks back, drawing on his football experience as a highschool quarterback in tight situations.

"Lowe, I had a wide-receiver once. Said the same fucking thing every time we had third and ten. He never got in the open when it mattered, always cryin' about being left out of the play. Know what I'm saying?"

"Not really."

"Just stay by the car and watch the fucking bird."

He walks back to Katrinna and Jerry watches them enter the clinic. But he is not to stay by the car, or watch the bird, a heat-score if there ever was one. He walks out of the parking lot to the street. He needs a sign.

A few slate-grey furrows of dark cloud intercept the sun, then break and move on. A beam of sunlight comes down, comes down and falls on the one and only beer parlour across the street. He crosses, finishes his smoke and dives inside.

He blinks, blinded for a moment. Underfoot, the comforting softness of thick carpet, in the air the stale smell of beer, smoke, and a hint of the harder stuff. Soft jazz pulsing from overhead speakers as dim red lights show the way. A cabaret sadness that at the same time bespeaks a kind of joy. And the promise of a drink. Must hang a red light over dead Grandma's sofa when back at the place, to settle the nerves and bolster one's usual state of melancholy. On now to a table, covered in dark cloth. A sign: "Reserved." Sit down anyway. And order fifty, the end could well be near. And settle with one's back to the wall, one's eyes to the door ("The world is pocked with these invidious openings, behind which lurk the recidivists," a somewhat educated older junkie had once told him).

A waitress seen moving through the red hush, like a dolphin at play on her tail, he thinks, her white blouse the tops of the waves. Balance that tray on your nose, sweet lady, the world teeters outside. And one will try hard not to think of dirty deeds or noisy half-mad birds from Geelvink Bay. Or out there, the rust-primered shitbox parked so conspicuously in the parking lot of the methadone doctor's office.

The waitress placing the ten glasses as requested doesn't appear surprised. Has seen it all. Some drops of liquid spill and expand in a darkening circle on the dark cloth. An amused look and she leaves, a measured, pleasurable gait. He smiles back. And best plunge one's whole head into this first glass of beer, pretend to go down and rest on the bottom. Be one with the four-hundred-dollar fishes of Hector Lake that he so generously stole for his brother, pants bulging with plastic bags full of water, all orime's the same. Don't cry out, you've hopefully left the piranha back in the tank and they're not now thrashing at your balls, the store clerk suspicious as you try to make for the door without spilling, without spilling all the beans.

Empty glasses are moved to the far side of the table as the full ones make their way to the near side. An hour or more passes although he's not really marking the time, there's no point, he isn't in control. And what's happened to Hector Lake and Katrinna Reticuli, he can't help wondering while staring into the bottom of a glass now tipped back, the glass and his hand concealing his face. Are there echos in here, of breathing. Cries of old sailors. *We come on the Sloop John B, oh, how I want to go home*, light bouncing through the upturned foam-soaked prism of the glass, disjointed shapes breaking apart through the thick glass of the bottom. And unfuckingmistakable, breaking apart or not, the form of Hector Lake appearing through the thick foamed glass, for a moment filling the doorway to the outside. A black shroud, thinks Jerry, against the dying light of day. And the table's still covered with beers, only thirty-nine to go.

Hector stands over the table counting the empties.

"Christ. You expecting the whole team or what?"

"Where's Katrinna?"

"Where the hell were you is more like it. Give me one of those. We were looking all over. Had to wait. Wanted to go for a coffee. Katrinna's back in the clinic. She's having trouble pissing for her sample. You may have to piss for her."

Been doing that since the morning, thinks Jerry, and why is it no one in the junkie's exclusive seedy world ever seems able to pee when they have to?

Hector Lake stares at him across the table.

"You're pretty quiet."

"I'm okay."

"Well, I'm not worried about you but Katrinna is. Nobody's going to notice the bird if that's what you're thinking."

Jerry puts down an empty and slides it to the far side of the table, now Hector Lake's side, and grabs a full one. And that, Mr. Lake, may be truer than you think, for who on God's lonely dark earth cares about the bird? No, first they'll notice the rust-primered shitbox in all its glory, which the police know anyway, with no brakes, no horn, no taillight, no nothin'. Then they'll notice Hector Moses Lake and Katrinna Reticuli, known drug users and in possession of stolen goods worth over a thousand dollars (makes it a felony). And then there'll be only one thing left to notice, madly feigning innocence on the sidewalk. And that will be Jerry Lowe, Mr. Lake. Then they'll notice Jerry Lowe. An odd question strikes him and he's surprised he hasn't asked it before.

"Hector—Mr. Lake—I was just wondering. What, exactly, if anything, do you worry about? I don't think I've ever actually asked you. You told me you could have played pro ball. You had your own place when you were eighteen. And you're not stupid. Does that worry you at all? It kind of worries me, about myself I mean. I worry about things like that every day, all day, I think."

Hector Lake finishes a beer, absently reading the small bar menu on the table. He looks a little put out, not prepared for this "delving" kind of stuff.

"I worry about things. Worry like a bastard. Sometimes I wonder what I'm doing. Think I like running around trying to score, going to jail every six months? I'm out now but I still got three more charges coming up. It's crazy, I know. But all I really got to worry about is getting through the day. It seems it's only that now. Just the day. And what's your problem? You're not even a doper."

"What's that got to do with anything?"

"Well, you should be is all I'm saying."

Jerry Lowe drinks, two swallows. Hector may have a point.

"Maybe I'm nuts."

"I've thought about that too," says Hector Lake.

Jerry leans back in his chair, fingers drum on the table.

The red hush doesn't feel as safe anymore, and he needs a smoke.

"Fear, I think. Everything comes down to fear," Jerry says and Hector looks confused, then panicky. How did this start, this mindless mind-stuff?

The empty glasses are piling up and Jerry can't figure where it's all going. Come on, Katrinna over there. Piss. So everyone can go home. In his mind's eye, Katrinna with legs apart, squatting over the specimen jar. And oh, to be that jar, under the pink pudenda.

The waitress clears the empties and drops full ones. Hector Lake keeps talking, disjointed conversation about past escapades on the street and in the joint in an effort to stay away from that other kind of talk. Jerry Lowe tunes in and out, the pleasant mood of his refuge having changed. Katrinna comes through the door. She was finally able to pee and get her dose of meth and managed with a phone call from the booth across the street to set up a dope sell for later that evening. This motivates Hector Lake, who leaps up and begins making phone calls at the pay phone by the door. The bar is filling up with the after-office crowd and Jerry downs the second-to-last beer. It's still safer in the bar, feet sunk into the carpet under the red lights, than it would be outside. Hector Lake finishes his calls and waits by the door, signalling them it's time to leave. Jerry insists on not chugging the last beer, reluctant to follow.

Once outside his anxieties of the day rush back. The sun has gone down and street lights have come on. This is somewhat better, though, he thinks, and breathes a silent prayer—Thank you, sun. Under cover of night we will hurry home and I am afraid of one million things at this one moment alone and I can only pray, dear Lord, the white birdie it don't glow in the dark.

Moments later he cranks the shitbox into the liquor store parking lot, ignoring Hector Lake and Katrinna Reticuli who now want what he's wanted all along, to get home and meet with The Man and have a quick end to the whole deal.

He moves quickly into the store, pauses dazzled at the door. Yeow. After the red hush of the bar and the waning light outside these lights are blazing. Any paranoia one may be suffering is up ten to twenty percent when under the naked glare of fluorescent lighting. Hand out name tags why don't they, so everyone can know who and what you are. And down the aisle on the far side, quickly, shelves on either side stacked high with tenuous well-being—and what are these other people doing? He dodges a man and woman standing in the aisle—they're browsing—good lord, who can spare the minutes staring at labels, pursing lips? Further on, the aisle blocked by a guy who doesn't know his arse from a hole in the ground, bending over and reading labels along the bottom shelf. A temptation to just kick him in the ass, send him head-first into the cheap wines he's contemplating. At the whisky section and standing slumped in front of the brand you want is an old geezer tapping his chin. Tap away, man, make no mistakes. Get the right thing, big decisions everywhere being made. On what best to drain to the bottom this night to forget the evils of the week. And reaching over the geezer's shoulder wanting to bonk him hard with your elbow to snap him out of whatever stupor he's in, clutching a forty-ouncer tightly to the cashier lineup where you're hit with an irresistible urge to just barge ahead waving money. A delicate situation now, don't fumble change pieces, call attention to yourself. The unfriendly eyes of the cashier man, under which all one's secrets are laid bare. And there's been thirteen undercover cops spotted in there already, make no mistake, all of them pretending to shop for booze, one eye staring straight ahead at a gallon of Fucked Duck while the other searches the aisles for bird thieves. And while fumbling your change pieces a glance at the door and number fourteen undercover cop coming in. A clever disguise, an old lady in a green hat carrying a shopping bag, Sergeant Aunt Matilda, probably packing a radio and a .38. Check one's hair and clothing for feathers, the cops are sticklers for clues. And it isn't easy heading for the door while walking on eggshells.

So it's this whisky Hector Lake swigs while chatting it up with Katrinna as they crawl their way through the rush-hour traffic. At this pace Jerry Lowe can close his eyes for a moment. The traffic may not be moving but his nervous system is. Some form of fear, it seems, is always close, tingling and scratching along underneath the surface when not outright bubbling along the top of it. Even when younger, everything seemed fearful. Girls. The dark. Oral book reports. And the road down can start innocently enough. The pilfering of candy from the corner store, money from the top drawer of the folks' dresser. Those early experiences of one's step into banditry, now resurrected in later years, on, of all things, knocking over pet stores to help one's junkie friends. And a long way off now those aseptic ice cream shopping malls of a guy's middle-class liberal past.

There was fear even at the university, propounded by those supposedly in the know to be those "carefree days of college." The fear that if you didn't get that higher education you'd die an auto mechanic or something. And that would be so bad? And how he'd identified with those rats in second year psych-lab, running blindly through the mazes to be zapped or not depending on their choices. And who could forget staring bravely out across the campus when told by your girlfriend she was pregnant, not learning until later it was all hysteria but willing then to do the noble thing and drop out, step off the platform of higher education and plummet to the pot-holed poorly kept roads of the labour force, the whole affair taking years off your life. And was that the top of the hill then, those days, with no direction left to go but down, maybe, like it certainly seems one has done.

    He's aware of Hector beside him, seemingly content with downward spirals, bouncing the forty-ouncer on his lap. And it isn't important right now what choices one has made. No, just getting that bird home is, and hoping the whisky hits the spot, hoping it hits that spot, baby, where beats the dull throb of a nebulous cranky world.

He climbs the road above the house. It's hot and dusty, his feet already sweating through his socks in his sneakers. The road ends abruptly at the tree line, there are no more houses beyond. He crosses the rocky stream on the right and keeps climbing through bush following the swath of the power lines. A thick wall of fir and pine rises on either side. Deer frequently come down as far as the water-shed fence and are sometimes seen on this side of it, wandering the newly cleared lots below. Whether there's a hole in the fence somewhere or they manage to jump it he doesn't know.

He got the pellet rifle three days ago for his twelfth birthday. It's got an eagle head embossed on its stock and has a slightly larger calibre than most other pellet rifles he's seen other kids use. You have to aim low, the sights are off a bit and not adjustable. He has ten pellets in his pocket and one in the chamber.

He moves up the slope wading through brush that is waist high. The air buzzes with the sounds of insects and bugs can be seen dancing through the light around his head. He slings the rifle in one hand and scrambles up the loose soil, the thick brush tugging at his jeans. A hundred yards up from the creek a wild flutter erupts on his right. A brown blurry ball rises out of the scrub and flies a short distance, then drops out of sight. Another blurry ball rises on his left and skims the tops of the bushes veering wildly across his path and it too drops from sight into a yellow thicket of scotch broom. He's startled, his sneakers fighting for a foothold on the rocky soil under the brush. Running is impossible although his first instinct is to do just that. About ten yards ahead, a dead tree lies across the way, the white heads of toadstools sticking out along its grey flank. He sees the grouse, until now invisible, nestled on the top of the log. It's facing him, its chest puffed out like a football below its head and only its head is moving, quick jerks from side to side.

He raises the rifle. He can feel his heart pounding. Sights to a spot just below the centre of the football and pulls the trigger. There's no retort, just a ping followed by a loud WHUMP! The bird doesn't move.

He reloads, snapping the chamber open and fumbling for another pellet in his pocket. He moves closer keeping his eyes on the bird. He aims again and pulls the trigger. Again there's a ping followed by a WHUMP! as the pellet connects with the football. The bird still doesn't move for an instant, then suddenly lifts off and flies down the slope toward him in a rush of wings. He drops to his knees in the brush and feels the air above his head pound as it passes inches overhead. When he turns around to look down the slope there's nothing. A thick branch high on a fir below him waves violently, then settles. He stares up at it and thinks he can see the football through the branches and it's a good thirty yards away if not more.

He thumbs another pellet into the chamber not caring anymore about noise or sudden movement. He raises the rifle, sighting just below the branch and pulls the trigger. There's the ping sound followed this time by a THWAP! as the branch waves crazily and something falls through the shadows to the base of the tree and remains still.

There's no sound save the buzzing of insects. Sweat runs down his face. He's trembling for some reason and stares at the dark hole that is the base of the tree. He can't advance into it. Not alone.

He scrambles through the brush back down the slope.

9

White-dick Kids

SINGH SIDHU'S MIND, NOT UNLIKE JERRY LOWE'S, is prone to call up quotes when in any state of heightened fear or euphoria, although, unlike Jerry Lowe's, Singh's mind will more often than not be unable to pinpoint where they actually come from. The quote, "She who is born a beauty is half married," which rockets out of nowhere while he sits in the beer parlour, is almost a blessing, for if Shashi Bhattal is anything, she isn't a beauty. This should bring him some relief, but it doesn't. He feels alone, just him and The Fear. And Shashi Bhattal, wherever she is, is alone too in a sense, powerless over his wayward and now beer-fed imagination. Throughout the last hour or so she's been equipped with the face of a Chinese dragon, the disposition of a Java wart snake and the brain of an Indian water lizard. In all, no better than a triceratops, until now long thought extinct, but through the power of beer and despair vividly brought back to life by Singh Sidhu.

 An empty beer glass. White globules of foam lay up along the sides. He hunches forward, peers into it, conjuring a desolate dried-up beach where in a later drunkenly written poem it will, of course, symbolize his young life, and where some day all too soon he may be taking his and Mrs. Shashi Singh Sidhu's kids, all nineteen or more of them. His father looks happy, though, he's on the beach too in colourful shirt and shorts, quietly pulling the strings.

The jukebox stops playing and louder music booms through the bar. He looks up, waitresses have just as abruptly appeared, or so it seems to Singh. They weren't there a minute ago. And carrying trays that appear stacked with glasses ten high and moving with deadly efficiency between the tables. The place is packed now and Jagit and the brother younger are no longer playing pool and have returned to the table. Evening has somehow descended, sneaking up unnoticed in the windowless confines of the bar.

He signals madly, better get some more beer fast before it's all taken. A flash of bright light—he blinks—and stares up at the golfball lights that have lit up around the floor of the stage. He looks higher and sees sequins and lace, two muscular tanned legs growing into hard swaying curves. On the lower ends of those supporting legs, catching his eye, two delicate high-heeled feet flash through the golfball lights. The Fear has once again gripped him, he wants to talk to Jagit. But—HEY, MOMMA—he stops thinking about it. A stripper bathed in reds and golds, crotch bared and circling the air above his head. Talk has its place and it's not here and now, whisked away on the hardened points of those tits that are pointing straight to the heavens. And who cares about cares, or heaven for that matter. He's witnessing a miracle being performed right here on Earth.

Above him the body of reds and golds shudders and rolls

to the music. Shudder. Roll. Shudder. Roll. Words come to mind. Smash it. Crash it. Wrap it around the bedpost, throw it out the door. The earthly miracle above him bending over, unfearing and jutting a naked rear of red and gold out over their pointed heads, bright moon and sun, all rolled into one. And creeping slowly around, fingers, crimson-tipped, cheeks of bum pulled wide apart, no map needed, the treasure's there, gentlemen, for all to see. And Jagit Sanghera, the brother younger and Singh Sidhu, their faces raised into the red and golden light, blushing honours, in one loving obscene gaze.

From the brother younger comes a yell of triumph, he is indeed getting a hard-on.

Thump. Thump. Boom. Boom. Rock. Now roll.

Singh Sidhu pounds the table, finds himself staring smack-dab into the pink opening—Hari Rama, Alabama—don't close—it's all for me.

He mishandles a beer, foam puddling out in a pattern from which he takes a quick Rorschach Test. Everything looks like tail, and maybe it's better to allow himself this one last hard-on, one last jaw-breaker while still a free man. An image—a cock—it must be his—engorged to the ceiling and letting loose a last load of liberty, then coming down in all its force on top of one's lecherous skull. Not even married yet but already knowing he will be unfaithful.

Another cry from the brother younger, "LOOKIT THAT!"

"OYEE, YOYEE!" from Jagit. "DRIVE THE GREEN BEHEMOTH UP THAT, EH MAN?"

Singh sobers somewhat at this last remark from Jagit Sanghera. How can anyone feel aroused at such a numbskull and infantile suggestion? But he does. He feels uneasy, perhaps within him lies some hidden sickness, a dark perversion, a gene in the wrong place or worse, not even there at all.

"WHAT'S SHE PUTTIN' UP THERE!"

"O GOD!"

"O BABY!"

He proffers a private toast, raising his glass toward the dancer above. A toast to this dance of naked flesh that can so ably numb some senses while arousing these others. And to the triceratops once more extinct. And he again believes there is a heaven. Maybe all will be well, you just need a little faith. He gulps some beer, envisions an uncertain future, and lends his support, his voice lost in the din of the bar.

"Keep . . . praying . . . boys . . ."

The dancer finishes, those two pointed breasts taking a bow. And one last glimpse of forbidden regions. The brother younger is still swept up.

"Let's go kick the shit out of somebody!"

Jagit Sanghera looks at him with sibling pride. Singh Sidhu proffers another toast. To life, so merry. To *sajjania*. And thus, predictably, to tail. And nothing, he thinks, gets any better than this.

But the good feeling doesn't last as Jagit Sanghera inadvertently makes some comment about Singh's father and established customs. Joking, of course, but not funny. The brother younger leans forward eager for more news. Singh keeps watching the golfball lights trying to regain the moment.

"I don't feel like talking about it anymore."

"Well, it could just kill you, man," says Jagit Sanghera.

"Come off it."

"No shit, Singh. We had a cousin. He didn't want to get married either. A pre-arranged thing just like you. They finished the vows and he lasted ten minutes. Then dropped dead right after loading his plate with the chicken tikka and gobi!"

"Bullshit."

"It's the truth! I remember the plate hitting the floor, man!"

Some theories then propounded by the two brothers on how to possibly throw a monkey-wrench into any pre-arranged marriage plans. Some form of dishonour is needed, some act, violent or obscene, that can offend the bride's family. Singh Sidhu begins to feel better, through acts of gross indecency lie hope, and all may as yet not be lost.

The music booms again. A new set of high heels spin through the golfball lights, a black miracle this time. He sinks back in his chair, will do like the astronauts do when they blast off. Say, *Mary had a little lamb*, keep reciting. They do that to keep their chests from caving in, as this dancer's will never do. Muscles stretch and coil above him. Hot tar. The patrons should be given special pressurized suits to wear, to keep the gases and blood flowing. He again mishandles a beer, droplets dribbling down his chin. A sign of the times; everyone's a slob. Through gross indecency does lie hope, and possibly the fulfillment of one's dreams.

The lights on the stage switch to blue, blue on black skin, like a knife sheath. Rock. Roll. *Boom. Boom*. He stares up at the stage, so many things in the world are held sacred, why not the plied-apart orifice? And Pop, wherever you are, if you could just get an eyeful, just an eyeful of this action, you would ask your son's forgiveness. Your eyes would fill, poetically, father, just like you like to think, with tears of joy and sadness, joy for the naked dancing babe above, sadness cuz you'll never get a piece of it. You'd probably see the sweat glistening on her skin as melted silver religious icons or some fucking thing, but it doesn't matter. It's okay to dream, father. If you don't believe me, just look at this mother bulge in your young son's pants. Could pound incense sticks into the floor like fence posts.

He gasps for air, unaware he's been holding his breath. Is it The Fear or something more seedy? Above, the miracle grins down, white teeth, a chomping half-moon. Damp breasts swing. His face takes on a regal expression, thinking everyone else must be drunk. Let me and my time be buried here in this hell-hole, dark crotch bobbing, reeling—goddamnit, it's diving—quiver, quaver, bottomless love-pits, everything godless and obscene, Singh Sidhu will protect you . . .

He allows his mouth to fall open like everyone else's upon seeing the black hands go there, reaching down where no one else dares. His throat is dry even as he drowns it with beer. The black hands pull apart, revealing all that's pink and holy, all that's the main reason for any young man to stay unattached during one's youthful years, and he's sure he sees a light burning at the end of that tunnel.

We've all had it now, he calls to himself, bury your heads in the ground you other gross foul ugly pigs, heads in the ground, only to have something else stick up and face the world.

The second show ends and they grope for the door. It's time to leave, head out for fresher dimly lit rooms. Outside a brisk evening breeze blows across the parking lot. They walk unsteadily to the car, Jagit Sanghera describing a fantasy liaison he would like to have with that last stripper. The Green Behemoth roars to life and Singh Sidhu manoeuvres it out of the lot and onto the street. He's not feeling too badly, the music, beer, and the strip shows having somehow put some distance between him and any impending personal disasters. They've been pushed away, he feels insulated for the moment, safe. Jagit Sanghera cranks the music.

They roar onto the viaduct toward the East End and Jagit doesn't mention Singh's speed this time. All three are thin, light of build, between five-six and five-ten in height. For Singh Sidhu and Jagit Sanghera, being evening, it's stiletto-nose boots, low-cut, black leather, zippers up the side. For the brother younger it's Saucony Grid OTR Plus pin-striped runners night and day. All wear Ripzone two-tone oversized T-shirts of different colours with a Point Zero hoody for the brother younger, Columbia Roc cotton canvas jackets for Singh and Jagit. Firefly Quinn Twill cargo pants on all and Sundog "10.28" Ultraflex sunglasses.

Mid-way across the viaduct the brother younger leans forward from the back seat.

"Did anyone see what they had in there?"

Jagit turns around trying to see out the back window.

"Where?"

"In the back of that Volkswagen bug back there. It was in the back. White. And seemed to be going nuts . . ."

"Those white guys?"

"Yeah."

"Probably one of their white-dick kids."

"But it was caged."

"That's what they do."

Laughter erupts in the Green Behemoth, as somewhere above, the moon careens a line with the sun, looking heated in the night sky.

10

Dingbat Teasers

SOMETIME THAT SAME AFTERNOON that a cockatoo goes missing from Delgado's Pet Mart on the Delta, at the Shell carwash and gas station at Second and Main in Vancouver, Conrad Parker stretches over the hood of a red Mustang at the full-service pumps, his spindly arm moving out like a spider's leg to wipe down the windshield. A huge yellow scallop revolves high on a pole at the corner of the lot glinting in the sun. A bell sounds from the pump and the pungent odour of gasoline fills his nostrils. Oil-greased and well-chewed fingers replace the gas cap, one finger reaching up to scratch his nose. He circles to the driver's window.

A woman, middle-aged and cosmetically tanned, wearing a low-cut tight-fitting dress, offers her credit card. Conrad Parker stares at a thin blue vein that pulses on her neck as she notices the pimple festering on his.

He takes the card, attempting a smile, managing a leer. His eyes drop to the gap of her breasts as his mind steams out on its familiar course. His world tends to be an internal one, one filled with twenty-odd years of fantasies mixed with the inevitable disappointments of good fantasies gone bad. Right now the fantasy is maybe a quickie through the carwash with the tight-fitting dress. Why not, it happens, happens all the time. Best not even to think about the consequences, just go for it. Shove the old hand right down that soft inviting cleavage. Drive the old wang-dang hard and deep into the wanting pink lagoon. Take her right on the seat, those tanned legs kicking the air, heels going right through the roof, could probably get away with it too with this obviously bored housewife, horny as the day is long.

He returns her card, holding the receipt low for a signature and a closer look. Maybe a lucky brush of knuckles on those you-know-whats.

She smiles. "Thank you."

Conrad Parker smiles back, but looks instead like he's hurt himself. And strains to hear the unsaid message, the hidden go-signal.

Thank you, she said. That's what she said.

The Mustang turns out of the lot leaving him standing by the pumps, a visible sagging taking place within his coveralls as he watches it go. Motionless and standing in worn Columbia "Broken Trail" outdoor shoes and, under the coveralls, a threadbare hockey jersey, faded low-end jeans.

He should have gone for it. And just what is it with these women, aging holier-than-thou broads showing tits and ass. Dingbat teasers—"Look at me, my body's a goddamned holy temple." Well, forget it, lady. I'm onto it. I'm onto your game.

The phone rings in the station office. He crosses the island and goes inside. The voice of the young Mrs. Parker comes over the line as he watches a muddied Ford Bronco through the window pull in and honk its horn at the far pumps, two short quick toots. He ignores it. Over the telephone the young voice of Shirley Parker crackles, something about a bill to be paid, some groceries to be picked up. Some endearments of a normal domestic life, Conrad Parker barely listening and pulling hard on a cigarette, ignoring too, the No Smoking sign. Two more toots from the Bronco, the sound mingling with the swish of traffic along Main.

What the fuck is that asshole doing?

Leaning to the doorway, putting his hand over the mouthpiece.

"That's the self-serve pump!" Asshole.

The driver of the Bronco smiles and waves as the motor starts and it begins backing away.

Conrad Parker puts the phone back to his ear. Good fucking riddance, go somewhere else.

The Bronco comes forward again.

"Fucker's pulling in to the full-service pumps—I don't fucking believe it!"

"What was that, honey?"

"Ah . . . nothing."

"Did you get all that?"

"Yeah, I got it. Got to go."

He manages, with effort, a civilized demeanor while crossing to the Bronco. Service with a smile. Lift the hood, check those oils. Above the canopy seagulls knife through the air fighting for perches atop the yellow scallop, their high-pitched cries one more thing to grate his nerves. Under the upraised hood of the Bronco he finds a dull peace, head hidden among machine parts. The engine wells of vehicles have become of late a place where the world can take a powder for a moment, a place where his mind can be allowed a second or two to settle, numb out and imagine a better world, for him, not a better world in general. But it doesn't always work as in this case thoughts of a new baby on the way, unpaid bills and recently phoned in and already forgotten grocery lists intrude on his peace. A sick desire to just lay his head on some sharp moving part of the engine, not that they have them anymore, and holler out a polite request of Smiley there behind the wheel to turn over, please, the motor.

He emerges from under the hood, pushing it gently but firmly down with his elbows, greasy hands kept visible in the air to show the cheery smile behind the wheel that someone cares not to make a mess of things.

The Bronco pulls out leaving him standing a moment beside the pumps again, and again, it appears, deflating. His face and arms catch the sun, he's forgotten he's still smiling. To an onlooker it might seem maybe, almost, that the guy is about to imbibe in some small personal celebration of the world, maybe glance around to establish that all is well and evolving rightly. Because the guy stands there quite a while, not moving.

But that's not really happening, only Conrad Parker knows, and he snaps out of it and ferrets another cigarette from his pocket while vacantly continuing to read for the thousandth or more time the helpful driving hints and homilies hung on signs about the lot. Buckle Up! Redeem Competitor's Coupons Here. Serve Yourself Crystal Clear Ice—*BRRRRRRRR!*

He steps quickly into the station office, skewering a receipt on a small spike, and hunkers down behind a hanging bastion of automotive paraphernalia and an impregnable wall of tires piled against the window. A name tag rises and falls on his chest: Conrad Parker, Assistant Manager.

The clock says ten forty-five and it's time to begin wondering where is the goofy, doddling dough-head Luther, Luther the retard? Supposed to be here half an hour ago to open the carwash, free with any fill-up. Late again. Lucky he's the nephew of the regional boss or something which makes him immune from getting in the soup for screwing up, which he does plenty. And it was weird at first, working with a retard. The boss said he was 'slow,' but a good boy. And Luther does seem harmless enough. And always does show up eventually, doddling onto the lot, staring a few minutes down at the tulips planted around the grass meridian at the pull-in. Then a stop at the air pump further on and staring at it. The vacuum hose will get a look. Then raising his eyes to the sky, and some mornings, it seems to Conrad Parker, staring right past that into space and possibly beyond. Then finally he will make his way over to the antiquated carwash where the familiar scenario will begin. Windows left down when sending through the cars. The moving drag chain hooked up with the emergency brake still on and that 'ping' sound of another drag chain breaking, suds from the soap rollers somehow in his hair and on his clothes even before the first car goes through the wash. And then there's that smile. No matter what crisis, that Luther smile. If anything in the whole scenario is more unsettling to Conrad Parker, it's that constant Luther smile. Through thick and thin, it's there. And the biggest mystery of all to him is how can anyone possessed with what appears to be so little seem so freaking happy all the time? The closest he's been to an answer was supplied one morning by the restroom wall, where, somewhere between the various renditions of cocks, twats, and balls, someone had scrawled, "There is a pleasure none but madmen know."

He chances a peek over the wall of tires. Another car has pulled in to the full-service pumps, another lazy bugger. He continues smoking out to the gas pumps, flicks the butt along the ground into some purple-green stains of gasoline. Some gulls, one moment sitting atop the yellow scallop, instantaneously start shrieking and circle in a pack down to the lot. A half-eaten hamburger and french fries spin through the air onto the lot, the car they came from racing up Main Street. Deep-rooted resentments and frustrations peak, undefined upon any specific object, much akin to the pressure generated in a can of pork and beans he'd heated on a hotel room radiator only eight months before while newly arrived in town to get this job. That had been a mistake, resulting in walls and bedspread covered in dizzying designs of beans and tomato sauce foreboding ill even then of he and the new wife moving out to the coast, he licking tomato sauce from a sleeve in between poundings on the hotel room door, a voice on the other side shouting that there were only ten minutes—ten minutes to leave or clean up the mess!

He mishandles the radiator cap and it spins across the pavement, the gulls going for it, Conrad Parker chasing. Get away you bastards. Get away from that radiator cap.

The car when ready pulls out in a hurry, the gulls again swooping and shrieking onto the lot fighting over burger, bun, and french fries. Swooping and looping, Conrad Parker stooping to pick up a rag. And throw it down again. Someone else has just pulled in wanting a fill-up and a wash. And where in fuck are you, Luther—pea-brain? One's gonna ball the next broad comes through here. Ball the next broad.

A seagull hopping through the purple-green stains of gasoline. Looks like it's leering, french fry dangling from its beak. Conrad Parker leering back, flicking his lighter. Cook this fucker's goose—get out of here, Gas Station Attendant Only.

Another gull swoops down, the two gulls fighting over the french fry. The foot of Conrad Parker drawing near and lashing out, the gulls shrieking, taking flight, Conrad Parker standing defiant by the gas pumps with the french fry in hand. And downs it in a bite.

11

Mad Is Bad

THE PUDGY FINGERS OF LUTHER THE RETARD (plump frame clothed in red Airwalk sweatshirt and pants with pinstripes, elastic waistband, large white sneakers) cradle the broken links of yet another hook-up chain, "Gone kaput." First there's that snapping 'ping' sound and then the pretty jingle-jangle. You can feel the sound almost, through your hands. Like tall grass can tickle. Like, the best feel of all, a handful of marbles. The carwash is open till late tonight and that's good, good for Luther. Likes all that water gushing, the hissing sounds. The furry rollers that look like big bears. Going round and round over the cars making them clean. So the cars squeak when rubbed. Squeak like mice. Like Mr. Skinner used to say in the hospital place, about dirt, crawling around in his pajamas on visitor's day on his hands and knees looking for cigarettes. Feet of Nurse all of a sudden in front of his nose. Mr. Skinner you'll get dirty, she'd say. And Mr. Skinner down there playing horsey, looking up. Miss, cleaniness is next to godliness, but dirt is indigenous to the spirit of man, he'd say. Mr. Skinner was always saying those funny things with the big words.

He looks over at the thin coveralled body of the angry man, Mr. Conrad, now leaning on them gas pumps. Smoking. With signs hung all over saying not to. No sense this makes to Luther. Can all go kaplooie. And Mr. Conrad always be saying those bad words when the cars come in. Says them again when the cars they go out. To feel that mad. Mad is bad. Luther should maybe give him one of these chains. Make that face all happy with the jingle-jangle. That'd do it. Better not. That face of Mr. Conrad not to look so hot every time there be a 'ping' breaking chain sound. Take the brake off and take it out of gear before hooking it up to the moving track, Einstein, Mr. Conrad sometimes says. And he's right. That's how it's done. And Mr. Conrad did bring a Coca-Cola over. Said not to pour any on the customers. That was a nice thing to do.

He watches a blue car pull in, and, like a blind fish rising from the deep, so do his hopes. He sucks harder on the cola.

Oh boy, this blue car it looks dirty. Maybe it'll want a carwash. Wish, wish. And hope.

He picks up a half of a baloney sandwich. Had given the other half to those dipping diving seagulls this day earlier, now all gone home. Down to the ocean where they snuggle together to keep warm and discuss the day. And he can hope that the ones that were here today, that said thanks for the sandwich, will tell the others about this guy Luther and his sandwiches. So more will come tomorrow.

Holding his sandwich in mid-bite. The boss, Mr. Conrad, is whistling a tune, sounding happy, his head down under that dusty blue car hood. This is something different, something scary. Better wait and see.

Under the dusty blue car hood Conrad Parker is thinking, not of Luther the retard and that last broken hook-up chain, but of all things, of his home in Red Deer, Alberta. And of Moncton, his best friend, the normal-sized son of the midgets, Mr. and Mrs. Buckingham, each but three-and-a-half and four feet tall. And how to his surprise Mrs. Buckingham had shed normal-sized tears when he and the new Mrs. Parker had left to come to the coast.

He stares at the engine, a little shaken. Affection is weird. The strange tugs and pulls that you feel when thoughts turn to friends and family in far-off places. Like Moncton and Mrs. Buckingham's tears. Like his own mother, long dead. And a dad back home booze-crazed with one dead wife and one married gone son. Unnerving what snakey crawly things can slink their way through your head out of the freaking blue. Jesus shit, a lot of that has been happening to him lately. It causes him to look over at Luther, which isn't reassuring. The retard looks like his eyes are gonna pop out and roll away. Really wants this car for the wash, poor bastard.

Luther's eyes do feel like they're gonna pop, open in terror at that thin coveralled body leaning itself down to that dirty car window. Oh, help. Mr. Conrad's saying something to that customer. Holy-moley, probably those bad words. Jeeps and creeps. Bad is bad. Calling the customer a jerkoff or something.

He holds still, the can of cola tipped to his lips, forgotten. Cheeks filling. Inside his mouth a fizzing, a volcano in there. Fizz. Fizz. Face contorting in another look of terror, pulling back from the can of pop gasping for air. Lordy—

nose, eyes, head and hair of Luther filled with the fizzing. Fizz. Fizz. Fizz everywhere.

He retches.

Holy-moley. Have exploded.

Through watery eyes he sees the thin coveralled body of Mr. Conrad straightening up from the dirty blue car window.

Luther hates you.

And waving over.

Luther didn't mean it.

Jeeps and creepers. A customer. So excited have forgot what to do. Re-wrap this baloney sandwich part, that's one thing. Get the can of fizzies well out of the way, away from the heads of the customers. Big belch of the fizzies—ow—can't move for a minute. Now all the things to remember. Release brake. Take out of gear. Before hooking up to the moving track. The track. Over and push this button, get the track a-rolling. And keep feet out of it. Watch pant cuffs, don't get them caught like the last time. No one can hear you once you're trapped in the carwash. Lucky, so lucky to be alive, is Luther. Scary in the rollers. Got all soapy and whacked good one time, made Luther's face red like an apple. Forgot behind the ears, was what Mr. Conrad said.

The blue car pulls around to the carwash. Conrad Parker sees Luther shuffling nervously back and forth and lends his silent support, "C'mon, goofball, you can do it."

Luther fidgets inside the car. Got to do this right. Release brake. There. Rattle this gear shift into the right place. Now get out and go around to the front, nice to hear this chain all jingle-jangle. Stick to business, Luther. Stay out of never-never-land when running the carwash, Mr. Conrad says. The tail end of this hook-up chain almost caught in that metal-toothed moving track growling at one's feet. Rip your fucking arm off, Mr. Conrad says. And he knows, he's the Boss. Watch all arms and legs, precious things. Don't want to walk on a peg, eat with hooks, says Mr. Conrad. Bend down under this dirty front bumper. Lots of mud here. Will do a good job, get all that mud. Reach up messy place. Hook up this one end. Now this other end of chain. Onto the metal-toothed moving track, growling so close to those fingies. Watch them too. Keep those fingies out of there.

Conrad Parker watches it all from a distance. Sees the slack in the hook-up chain taken up, comes the moment of truth, his eyes and the eyes of Luther the retard both glued to the chain, Luther's victory or doom written there. He sees the hook-up chain go taut and the blue car move slowly forward into the rollers, and—jesus, you could light up the whole fucking place with the look on that bozo's face.

The moment doesn't last, his teeth clamping down on his cigarette. Luther the retard can be seen advancing with the car as if attached, probably still wondering how he did it. A quick glance down to the customer who waits oblivious at the far end. Keep looking away, mister. Don't see this. Then looking back at Luther—what's he looking at? Where goest thou, poor dumb moron?

Luther into the rollers, met by a wall of water and taking a zonk on the bean from the rollers at the same time. Stepping back, dazed, as the car disappears into the wash, Conrad Parker rooting from the sidelines, "Don't fall *in*, you retard. Fall *out*." And Luther looking now to Conrad Parker like he's going to faint. Or fly away. Jesus lumbering assholes, the retard took quite a swack. Better get over there, hold up five fingers. See if he still knows his name.

The Crucial Struggle

12

Dog-eared Memories

THE SUN HAS LONG SET OVER the viaduct and wind whistles through a hole in the dashboard of the shitbox where something was once lodged, but Hector Lake is no longer concerned with any of the defects of the rust-primered shitbox. It's served its purpose and Jerry Lowe, not he, is driving. The forty-ouncer of whisky is propped on his knee and in the back seat Katrinna smokes a cigarette, seemingly oblivious to the bird that's still in a fit of panic, gnawing at its cage in the space behind her.

When Katrinna beats up her husband in the bathroom of their one-bedroom apartment in Montreal in 1970, she is not yet doing the hard drugs, nor even drinking very much either. She has a job, a secretarial position in the administration offices of McGill University. Ricky, her husband, is finishing up an economics major and although both are only twenty-one, it's decided they're in love and by all intents and purposes, marriage seems the logical, and, for both, the most secure next step. Katrinna has already learned to hide any insecurities under a veneer of toughness and independence, as is revealed in the bathroom that evening in a matter of heated seconds to her new husband Ricky. The party is well underway when it happens. The woman sitting on the toilet giggles as Ricky enters, her panties around her ankles and not bothering to hide her bare thighs. Ricky grins back, swaying left and right and blinking his eyes at her outspread legs. Enter then Katrinna, and needing only a glance to see where young husband Ricky's eyes are trying to focus. The first blow knocks him off balance and he falls sideways, dead weight, into the bathtub. Katrinna leaps in after, straddling his chest and pinning him there, small fists raining the blows down on the source of garbled pleadings and muddled apologies. The marriage and party break up immediately, Ricky being helped to a waiting car to stay a few days at a friend's place while Katrinna gets her things packed, some clothes and a few valuables, leaving everything else behind including the dog, which broke her heart more than any other part of the whole matter. On her own, enraged, she heads west leaving in her wake a relatively brief history so far of a restless and rebellious teenage spirit. She had been given over to the nuns when fourteen years old, after repeated attempts to run away, her parents always able to find her and bring her back, finally giving her to God hoping maybe a greater power could intervene where Child Services and the law had failed. So along with her bags and a few valuables, she carries west the memory of that incarceration, unaware of future ones, the longest being eighteen months in a minimum security facility on the West Coast for possession of heroin and a firearm in 1980, seventeen years later. The nuns will always travel with her, whether she's serving time in jail or working as a prostitute on the streets of Vancouver, to where she flees, like Hector Lake, on a warrant from San Francisco in '75. She will hear them pass in the hallways of run down hotels she calls home, see them open the door to her room and stand above her as she lies on the bed defiant and refusing to eat, their black robes making a rustling sound, like birds' wings, crucifixes hung from their necks and swinging like pendulums across their midriffs, the only flesh visible their faces and hands, those hands gesturing toward the food and then toward some undefined domain above them, above her, a domain she didn't for a minute believe, or ever would believe, was there.

She sees it first, the green Camaro suddenly roaring by on the left. Raising her head and catching a glimpse of a fast-moving chrome-bumpered rear that seems to ride higher than the top of the rust-primered shitbox. Some idiot is yelling something out the back window, she sees the chrome-bumpered rear cuts close across the nose of the shitbox. Jerry Lowe is forced to brake hard and Hector Lake grabs the hand grip on the dashboard.

"Asshole!"

"Christ!"

"Piss me off!"

"Let's not start losing it guys," she says. "So they cut you off. No big deal."

"NO BIG DEAL?" say Jerry Lowe and Hector Lake.

The traffic light at the end of the viaduct has turned red and they see the Camaro stop. Hector Lake leans forward.

"Get up beside those assholes when we turn the corner."

Katrinna sighs from the back seat and leans forward too. She's had her share of male egos, experienced the extremes they can go to from sheer mean aggression to wrapping themselves around her booted ankles as she tries to leave them, begging her in a pool of tears not to.

"I hope you assholes aren't forgetting what we're supposed to be doing. We got us a hot fucking bird here and we got to meet and dump it. Save your egos for another time."

Hector Lake looks blank—who the fuck said anything about egos?

"All we want is a look. We just wanna see these assholes."

They're a few cars behind but when the light changes they're able to turn the corner in the outside lane and pull abreast of the Camaro that's gotten boxed in behind a slow moving camper truck. A "Honk If You Love Jesus" sticker is barely discernible through the mud on the camper's rear bumper. The windows of the Camaro are rolled down. Hector Lake rolls down his window and looks across at the brown face rolling beside.

"HEY, ASSHOLE!"

Katrinna falls back in her seat, all too aware of the stunned silence that follows, the time it takes for whoever is in the Camaro to absorb the insult. In the side-view mirror of the camper ahead she can see the driver, an elderly man in a baseball cap, twist toward, and attempt to calm his passenger. And she will never know why or what makes Jerry Lowe do what at that moment he does, cranking the steering wheel to the right causing the side of the shitbox to meet the flawless green of the Camaro with the ugly sound of metal on metal.

The Camaro slows, some rust-coloured flakes left mingling with the metallic green down along the driver's door. Any more potential for verbal exchanges stops, swallowed up in another disbelieving silence. Even the bird stops squawking for a moment. Katrinna sees the camper truck pull away, an uncomprehending elderly face jiggling in each of the side-view mirrors, in one the mouth set, in the other the mouth open, a black hole gesticulating in the glass.

The camper gains some distance before taking a turn into a McDonald's up ahead, the two baseball caps treated to the sight of Hector Lake's face rolling by moments later hanging out of the rust-primered shitbox, a look of admiration apparent for this last maverick act of Jerry Lowe. And this, goddamnit (the look says), is what it's all about.

Katrinna grabs her shoulder bag. From the space behind her, a resurgence of screeches and the sound of beak chewing on metal. A few small white feathers float down in the air above her as she demands to be let out. Jerry is hunched forward over the wheel, possibly his only hope now being to motor blindly away from it all. He takes heart from Hector Lake who still beams with satisfaction beside him and doesn't appear too put-out by the questionable act of stupidity he's just pulled.

Katrinna again demands to be let out and he veers into the gas station at Second and Main.

"Okay! You want out? No problem!"

Katrinna doesn't answer but Hector Moses already has the door open and has leapt out to face the green Camaro that's screeched in behind them.

"Cut the crap, you guys. We got company!"

Jerry Lowe attempts and fails a garbled protest. His eyes are riveted on Hector Moses and the forty-ouncer of whisky now gripped club-like in Hector's hand under the gas station lights. A thin coveralled body can be seen standing beyond, hiding by the gas pumps trying not to be seen. And it's this way to nutsville and glory, boys, Jerry Lowe is thinking, things are happening way too fast.

Katrinna Reticuli, with boots kicking, is climbing out after Hector Lake. Jerry Lowe is out the driver's side, avoiding her gaze over the top of the shitbox. She doesn't wait long.

"See you at home, asshole."

Yes, I heard that, thinks Jerry Lowe, but will never admit it. Love is blind, and deaf. Got to find the arm of Hector Moses Lake in this sudden crowd of three guys, this crowd of three brown faces. Colour the arm muscular, and swinging an almost full forty-ouncer. Just follow those three leaping dodging bodies, those three brown heads are keeping clear of something.

He does some of his own leaping and dodging toward Hector Lake, attempting telepathy. Be still thy motherfucking hand, Hector, you bozo, we can take these guys without the forty-ouncer. We'll need it for the victory celebration.

He spies the bottle going skyward again, a blow intended for a brown head bobbing just beside him. He kicks out with a boot, causing the head to move aside. He can't suppress a shudder as the bottle whistles by. Too close. This rivals any craziness that has occurred earlier in the day. And Hector Moses Lake can be seen still moving and swinging the bottle, possibly pulling forth all his dog-eared memories of careening yellow Volkswagens, gridiron defeats, beautiful faces lanced by shattered glass and all the homeless years. But who cares about motivation and—jesus just how many of these Asian mothers are there?—the much-feared Asian hordes, feet whipping the air like a piss-tank centipede.

He backs up, tries some circling, Hector seems to have danced clear of the crowd, the main lead in this impromptu street production. He appears at home in the midst of the fray, now advancing again and moving boldly through and scattering his foes. It looks like there's three of these guys, Asian, the forty-ouncer once more seen brandished and the mind of Jerry Lowe again attempts telepathy, this time with more determination. But something else happens and he pauses in full stride, an idea from somewhere, a notion, from the back of his mind, an unknown well of common sense and self-preservation, a suggestion to get-that-fucking-bird-out-of-here, like now, man.

He forgets the forty-ouncer, can think only: Cops. They could come, they will come. With awkward questions, awkward questions and no answers.

He changes direction, heading back to the shitbox. One quick guilty look over to Hector Moses left standing against those three others, fighting on alone under the gas station lights, still swinging at dog-eared memories and the Asian hordes. Swing high and hard that whisky bottle, dear boy, we managed to drink some of it and don't spare the remaining thirty-four or so ounces if it helps secure a successful outcome to all this.

He pulls the shitbox out of the lot and rounds the corner down toward the train tracks failing to see Hector taking aim and releasing the bottle, the bottle whistling harmlessly through the air as one of the brown-faced guys ducks and the bottle lands in a shower of glass and whisky along the pavement. Jerry Lowe does, however, experience a sudden wave of bereavement and loss, not knowing why, as Hector Lake, back under the gas station lights, successfully connects with a boot in someone's stomach. It's then Hector hears Katrinna, taking her call at first as a call of support then quickly realizing otherwise. He glances around, for the first time noticing the conspicuous absence of the rust-primered shitbox and that chickenshit Jerry Lowe. Katrinna stands on the corner about to cross the street and he makes to follow. On the night air a distant siren can be heard as a brown face presents itself in front of him bobbing well within range of a roundhouse whallop, which he quickly delivers.

13

Amber Sloshing

SINGH SIDHU HAS READ: "The Indian mind has always been inclined to believe of itself that any power and wisdom thus attained, can only be so through the extremes of fasting, sleeplessness, beds of nails, burning coals and self-torment in general . . ."

"We must seem," he thinks, sitting behind the wheel of the Green Behemoth and waiting for the light to change at the end of the viaduct, "an insane race."

He's been tensing up again with The Fear, anticipating the inevitable, a meeting he will have to have with Singh Sidhu Senior about his future. It will be better maybe not to work the insanity angle of their race. Any mention of madness in or about the family has always seemed to precipitate just that from Singh Senior. A smarter approach may be to load on instead some high praise for the innate wisdom of one's people, regardless of how it's achieved. For was it not the people of his own race who tended to sit calmly on the tops of mountains to think things through while white guys just freaked out and gave away their sons while wandering the deserts and setting fire to bushes, nearly burning the whole joint down? And then there was that manna thing, manna from Heaven they say, that fell out of the sky. Some black shit and the Jews fucking ate it! Would a good Hindustani? A good Sikh? Not likely. It would have to seem obvious to anyone, especially the old man, that any good Indian, of any age, is more than capable of making up his own mind about things, of making his own life decisions. The old man would have to think about that. He'd have to.

The light changes and he guns the Green Behemoth off the viaduct, relieved to be moving again as a rust-primered VW bug comes up unnoticed in the left-hand lane. A face looks at him from the passenger side window and shouts something he can't make out. This in itself is not as startling as the eruption of outrage from Jagit Sanghera and the brother younger who have made out what was said and begin shouting back. Singh is forced to brake to keep from running into a camper truck doddling along ahead. It's at this moment the rust-primered VW side-swipes the Green Behemoth, a *KACHUNK* that Singh hears against his door and the sickening sound of metal against metal. He feels the bump, his eyes watching the ragged bumperless rear of the VW as it pulls away. The camper truck has somehow disappeared, the gap between the ragged end of the VW and the Green Behemoth widening. He pokes his head out the window and looks down and there, surfacing a sizeable scrape, rust-coloured flakes can be seen mingling with the green.

Jagit Sanghera is pounding his shoulder.

"Come on, Singh!"

"C'mon Singh! Let's get 'em, man!" yells the brother younger, his body halfway into the front seat.

Singh pulls in his head, still unbelieving. What sort of asshole would—he shifts down, his right foot tromping the gas pedal. The Green Behemoth leaps forward with a squeal of rubber just as the brother younger hollers, "He's turning in!"

The VW has pulled into a gas station up ahead and Singh Sidhu wheels the Green Behemoth in behind it. They lurch to a stop and begin piling out, Jagit Sanghera the first out of the car, his younger brother scrambling after him. Singh Sidhu leaps out his side and stands a moment by his open door. And thinks just maybe to pile back in again. A gargantuan muscle-bound white guy is approaching from the rust-primered VW swinging a whisky bottle. From out the other side of the VW comes another white guy, not too small either. For Singh Sidhu, any pride of self or race may have to wait. A silent apology to one's ancestors that discretion, while not exactly cowardice, may just be the smarter thing here, that bottle-swinging meatball is still coming and no matter what one decides—a good idea to steer clear at all costs that whisky bottle.

The brother younger, in contrast, appears to have no such doubts, moving forward. Dumb, but gutsy, thinks Singh Sidhu, as the brother younger leaps about, then takes a boot in the stomach from the muscle-bound white guy. Singh hears the expulsion of air, the brother younger doubling over and paying homage it seems to the tips of his shoes. Singh Sidhu then with a few tentative steps, a need for clear and fast thinking here. But this is hampered by the thousand beers consumed earlier. Fear is a state of mind, he thinks stupidly and not too clearly. So it's been said for generations by both East and West. And what a state one's mind is in. And then, thankfully, a more practical thought—always try to get behind bottle-swinging, muscle-bound yahoos.

He attempts this manoeuver, skirting to the right. Jagit Sanghera doing likewise but skirting left, Jagit looking the more determined perhaps because he has less on his mind altogether not having to contend with the horrors of an impending pre-arranged marriage and the consequent loss of his freedom. As for Jagit Sanghera, he does know one thing, and that is he would at this moment gladly marry a Kanpur junkie whore or even Shashi Bhattal for the loan of a baseball bat.

Singh Sidhu catches movement of a third person who has emerged from the VW—and oh, christ—great, a clown act, fifteen or more of these bastards are probably in there. But this one's a woman, who stands with her hands on her hips and glares at the two white guys, not at him.

He begins skulking in her direction, no whisky bottle visible or other weapons, only five-foot-two she is, but don't get cocky. Danger fucking lurks, even without much size and no weapons. Western women know how to bust their mens' balls, everyone knows.

He skulks back thinking it over—and christ, again—narrowly missing a frontal attack from the less muscle-bound white guy who's suddenly in his face. Fists and boots are directed at his head and balls, the white guy's eyes not focussed on him but on something above. The swish of something swooping down, smooth glass grazing his cheek and a glimpse of amber sloshing, and he isn't sure but thinks he hears a sigh of relief from the less muscle-bound white guy.

He backs up trying to get a wide-angle view. This isn't making sense. The less muscle-bound white guy is heading back to the rust-primered VW. The woman is shouting something and it's not endearments at less muscle-bound. Less muscle-bound is climbing into the front seat of the rust-primered VW, a blur of the caged white kid in back seen shrieking through the rear window. The brother younger has regained his composure but looks the wrong colour as the VW motors out of the lot and around the corner, leaving the muscle-bound white guy alone and the woman striding off without looking back.

Singh hesitates under the revolving yellow scallop—you need a fucking program to know what's going on here. Then again skulking—keep moving, muddle through. Sees the head of Jagit Sanghera ducking low, the whisky bottle passing over still wielded by the muscle-bound white guy. Whoosh. Baby. Close call, Jagit. That fucking monster scuzbag is still at it. Wants to kill us all. And pray that that thin guy in the coveralls just seen running into the gas station building is going to call the cops. Get someone here and some charges laid. And the muscle-bound *mengna* is again bearing down, and this is one way to beat the old ways, he thinks, assaulted with a deadly weapon, then you dance, and then you die.

He's no longer skulking. The face of the muscle-bound guy is before him, inches away, contorted, a bright red triceratops. Time to stand erect and flee. One can hear the voice of the woman drifting over from the street corner as the muscle-bound guy slows. The muscle-bound guy stops, listening. Singh Sidhu is again skulking, the muscle-bound guy sniffing the air. Singh Sidhu then standing erect, ready to flee. The muscle-bound guy turning and the whisky bottle released, aimed at the still wobbly head of the brother younger. The brother younger dropping low and the brown sloshing flying through the air doing cartwheels to finally smash on the pavement.

Oh shit, too close, thinks Singh Sidhu, too busy giving thanks for the spared head of the brother younger to spare his own. The night opens with a fist that meets the side of his skull. He crashes down hard onto the pavement seeing the muscle-bound guy turn and walk away. He stays in the sitting position where he lands too stunned to move and watches the shadow coming past from the revolving yellow Shell sign above. It flows over his outstretched legs, an inky liquid moving silently around to come again. Peaceful, almost pleasant here on one's bunghole gone numb. A siren can be heard on the night air, scuzbag justice, coming late after the call. Bring mops and buckets, officers, some order. He tries to focus and thinks he sees hands reaching down from out of the black moving liquid as it comes 'round again . . .

14

Bill-hooks and Scythes

CONRAD PARKER HAS WATCHED it all unfold between the white guys in the older-model Volkswagen bug and the Asian guys in the souped-up green Camaro. Only moments before the two cars screech onto the lot he has his head under the hood of a Ford Taurus, his boney finger idly flicking the wing-nut on the air cleaner. Might as well thump something too, he thinks, giving a good smack with a small socket wrench on the valve cover. That always sounds good. And loosen a few bolts and tighten them up again, make whoever's lolly-gagging behind the wheel think something out of whack has now been fixed.

He lowers the hood, this driver's smile in the Ford Taurus especially irritates him. Another happy bastard homeward bound, after a long hard day probably sitting behind a desk doing dick-all and getting paid for it. The night is cool, a crisp breeze funnels under the canopy rattling the safe driving signs. And he's come to terms with having to work an extra shift tonight. What the hell, he can use the overtime.

A limpid 'ping' comes from the carwash behind him, the 'ping' of a hook-up chain snapping. The 'ping' of, how many is it, the fourth hook-up chain breaking today? He shakes his head, hire the lonely and brain-dead, who pays for these chains? And why do assholes and retards live? What is the Great Plan the preacher was always thundering on about back home in Red Deer, Alberta, like he thundered, Do you Conrad Robert Parker take Shirley Margaret Konstanovitch as your lawfully wedded wife, and you thundered back, I DO, making the bride and the whole congregation jump, a life-sized statue of Jesus looking down from its place over the stained-glass window above.

He turns. Luther the retard can be seen at the carwash bending over the broken chain links, lifting them in pudgy fingers. The retard's hands are always trembling, his mind always in the clouds. And isn't it a simple enough fucking thing to do, to take a car through the carwash? Take the car out of gear, first? Then make sure the emergency brake's off before hooking it up to the moving track? His mind feels muddled, some things you just never understand. Like, is retardation contagious, that's what he would really like to know.

Luther is trying another chain, his body crouched down under the front end of a muddy Jeep Cherokee. Above him a sign advertises Hi-Glow Wax and Seal. The customer, Conrad Parker is relieved to see, stands waiting at the far end of the wash, out of the line of fire. And luckily unable to hear over the roar of the wash Luther grinding gears as he fights the Cherokee into neutral.

Conrad moves to the pop machine for something to do. His senses are heightened, coins dropping into the machine with a crash. The thud of the can coming down makes him jump. The carwash brushes roar a big brown blur and Luther the retard can be seen this time hooking the Cherokee up successfully to the moving track. "And now, dear God . . ." prays Conrad Parker.

The Cherokee enters the mayhem of steam and water, Conrad Parker gnawing his cigarette and checking the Cherokee's windows. Up or down? An eye again toward the Cherokee's owner at the other end of the carwash standing there in suit and tie, wrinkle free, looking casually over the lot. The poor bastard thinks everything's under control.

Luther the retard is floundering his way around to the customer end of the carwash, suds in his hair, something shining along his nose. He arrives at the other end, grinning at the Cherokee as it comes forth rolling slowly through the last rollers. He kicks at the hook-up chain. It comes free from the moving track, the Cherokee stops, unharmed. Conrad sees the triumphant smile on the retard's face, his pudgy hands running towels over the hood. The suit and tie goes over, says some kind words, Conrad Parker watching, that Luther grinning like he's going to burst for christ's sake.

And like what else? Like a loon, that's what.

Not being tuned into, or even interested in, the theories of cosmic causes and effects, Conrad Parker cannot surmise that gravitational pulls from the moon and straight lines of objects in space do not always herald the negative as might be expected, for what else can explain, especially on a day like this with an extra shift to work, the brief unguarded smile that crosses Conrad Parker's face, and the unguarded thought that maybe the fault isn't Luther's that he's a retard, and, even if he is a retard, he isn't a craphead, an asshole like so many who aren't even retards.

Having unwittingly forgiven an accident of Nature, he drops more coins into the pop machine. Will buy Luther his second Coke of the day for another successful run through the carwash. And really, given life's choices, its constant mind-numbing screw-ups, who would one rather work with—an asshole or a retard?

It's as he starts over to the carwash with the second Coke of the day for Luther that the Volkswagen screeches onto the lot, the passenger door opening even before it stops. And with another screech a souped-up Camaro tears in behind it.

He ducks back to the shelter of the pumps. The retard's on his own, he decides, have to watch what's happening here with a muscular guy leaping from the Volkswagen and waving a forty-ounce bottle of whisky. And, jesus, only assholes were known to drive cars all mashed up like that, rednecks from the backwoods. Mr. Buckingham drove something like it, all rust primer back terrorizing the quiet roads of Red Deer, Alberta. And he was crazy too. A Nash Rambler outfitted with specially raised pedals and seats, and Mr. Buckingham swearing they couldn't die of anything but natural causes. Too small a target, he'd say, young Conrad and Moncton crammed terrified in the space behind the front seats as Mr. Buckingham runs another red light while reciting:

"Little drops of water, little grains of sand,

Make the mighty ocean and the pleasant land,

So the little moments, humble though they be—"

"Little moments," thinks Conrad Parker. "Are there ever any?"

Another guy, less muscular, has emerged from the rust-primered VW and three guys have leapt from the Camaro, these guys thinner with brown faces. They all look drunk, he decides, evident by the confused movements of all five. But this isn't the end-all, it's not little enough. Things have to get bigger first. To his ears, from somewhere within the rust-primered VW, come sounds not quite human. And things beating. He crouches lower.

And, oh brother, he's always said what's a party without girls. A woman has climbed out of the VW and seems to be screaming at the two white guys; and all parties seem preparing for at least a three-way battle. He watches from the shelter of the gas pumps as the three brown-faced guys try to stay clear of the larger white one swinging the whisky bottle. There's shouting in two languages and a shirt is heard to tear. His gaze drifts back to the rust-primered VW and the madly moving shadows that can be seen through the back window. *Little drops of water, little grains of sand* . . . make little this moment.

He shifts, a cautious sidestep to get a quick look-see of the carwash. At the far end the Ford Taurus that he'd just serviced can be seen coming out, wet and riderless, rolling slowly but steadily on through the rollers. How the hell did that happen? And when? He wasn't even aware the guy in the Taurus wanted a wash. But, who cares, don't look. Let another hook-up chain meet its end, another customer stand there watching metal parts fly. A battle builds on the doorstep, and having to work late this night of all fucking nights.

But, in spite of the newer ugliness taking place, his attention remains riveted on the carwash. There's no sign of Luther the retard. Then he can be seen scurrying along the wash, towels in hand at the ready and in a foot race with that metal-toothed moving track. Bear down boy, lift those knees.

He estimates that Luther is gaining ground, the owner of the Ford Taurus standing at the far end thankfully still unaware of the drama. Luther huffing past the last rollers, neck-and-neck now with the headlights of the steadily rolling car, then with a final burst of speed kicking out at the hook-up chain only inches away from the moving track drive-wheel, where it's all disaster if he doesn't make it but he does, kicking free the chain.

Conrad Parker finds himself applauding silently from behind the gas pumps. He even thinks to call out, "Good work, you dizzy wacky bastard, but go call the cops. We got trouble!" But an image of the possible phone call, disjointed at best, on seagulls, furry rollers, bats in the belfry, negates that idea. He'll have to do it himself if he wants to be sure help comes. He readies himself to run, throwing a quick glance over his shoulder to the fight taking place under the revolving scallop. "Kick each other's heads in, boys, the more damage the better."

He sprints the short distance to the station building, flinging himself inside. Fumbling with the phone, misdialing. He calms himself, taking a deep breath—okay, now—manoeuvre fingertips correctly over these touch-tones. Jesus, they're making them smaller. Like everything else these days. Use a pen, some pointed object. And fast. Nine. One. One. How easy can it get? No jerkoffs are going to use this lot to screw up in this night. And all East Indians, it's known, carry bill-hooks and scythes. And all white idiot rednecks, plowshares and .45s.

Hello. Emergency. Big fight brewing at the Shell Station at Second and Main. Looks racial. Us against them. The retard just took a car successfully through the carwash and something is dying in the back seat of a rust-primered Volkswagen. Yes, I'm serious. And get here—fast.

He returns to the doorway. Christmasy sound of a bottle smashing, on someone's slow moving head he hopes. A glimpse of the Ford Taurus pulling out from the far end of the carwash—right—drive away—home to your lady and highball you high-hog chickenshit bastard. He sees Luther still mucking about at the far end of the wash, his fleshy hand squeezing a fiver. Jesus christ, that guy really rakes in the sympathy tips. A reward for surviving the tightrope once again, should walk Niagara Falls, that guy, on a metal-toothed moving track.

He turns back to the action taking place under the yellow scallop. The rust-primered VW and the smaller white guy have somehow disappeared. The three brown-faced guys are still leaping circles around the white muscular one, keeping out of his way. The big guy no longer has the whisky bottle but stands with shirt torn, swinging and kicking, holding them at bay. The woman can be heard calling from the intersection where she waits for the light. The big guy suddenly stops flailing and starts to shuffle after her. The brown-faced guys move in. A white muscled arm arches once under the lights and catches a brown head with a sharp swack. The brown-faced guy staggers and crumbles to the pavement hard on his butt as Conrad Parker winces from the shadows. Shouting erupts from the other two after the departing span of the big guy's shoulders, but they don't follow.

Conrad remains hidden in the doorway. The worst has

got to be over. Two of the brown-faced guys are still jumping up and down around the souped-up Camaro, the third standing dazed with his right hand rubbing his head, his left rubbing his arse.

He shuts the station door.

Jesus, is it over? And don't even wonder where the retard's gone, drying out somewhere, this dinghole Friday night. And don't dare to even light a cigarette for fear of being noticed. Three on a match, and bang, you're dead.

15

Pancake Man

SYLVAIN DEACON SHINES HIS FLASHLIGHT along the body. It lies face down, almost buried where they stand in the waterfront Municipal gravel pit at the foot of Wylie Street. About five-and-a-half feet long it looks, its back and shoulders sunk to the level of the ground like a cartoon victim run over by a steam roller, and, adding to the cartoon effect, along the length of its back is stamped a muddy tire mark. A bloody wound blackens the back of the head.

"Dump truck, maybe," says Sylvain Deacon.

Styler Ferguson gives a low whistle. It's been a long day and he's feeling it. "Christ, hardly have to bury the guy. Just stand on the poor bastard an' he's under. Flat as a pancake."

"What'd the security guy say?"

"Some kids found him. He doesn't know nothing."

They're silent a moment, staring down at the body. Bits of gravel can be heard rolling sporadically in the darkness, the mounds around them shifting, alive.

"Foul play you think?" says Styler Ferguson at last.

Sylvain Deacon snorts. Even in ugly and horrible moments

like this you can get a good one off. It's needed, now and then, like now, to ease the tension.

Styler Ferguson walks his toes into the beam of light. Sylvain Deacon stares at Ferguson's shoes. On the night air he thinks he detects a faint puke smell. It has been quite a day all right. That morning, after dealing with the naked woman on the rooftop, they'd stood in the alleyway behind the Drake Hotel, Ferg steadying a drunk who swayed beside him above a dapple motif of fresh vomit that shone off the surface of Styler Ferguson's shoe. Ferguson hoists the unsteady mass roughly into the paddy wagon—"It's in my sock!" Lifting a pant leg and extending his foot, Sylvain Deacon standing by, sympathetic to Ferg's plight after successfully avoiding the thousand piles of dog shit earlier that morning only for this. He looks around, reaches down and hands over the brown paper bag from the wino's bottle, Ferg tweezering it delicately between two fingers and attempting to wipe his shoe. A grizzled face presses itself to the inside of the tiny glass window of the paddy wagon and leers, a circle of misty cloud waxing and waning where it breathes.

Styler Ferguson's head snaps up, so hard Sylvain Deacon is sure he hears a bone pop. Ferg's jaw is at work, the muscles writhing and teeth clenched so tight that Sylvain Deacon is surprised any sound can come out at all.

"GET THAT COCKSUCKER OUTTA HERE OR SO HELP ME GOD!"

Sylvain Deacon signalling 'round to the driver. "Better be going."

The paddy wagon moving off, Sylvain Deacon taking a few steps forward. Ferg was losing it. And one more day, he had thought. One more day and no more back-alley drunks, bare-assed nutcases on rooftops or puke-filled shoes. He sees again the two of them, just him and Lucille, one long and lean, the other medium and full, hand in hand along white sand, maybe adjusting one's sunglasses to better see the bottle of white rum left to chill in a tidal pool, on its label two purple palms . . . but right now Ferg looks beyond pissed, he looks dangerous. His eyes are butter-balled to white globes and who can really tell Ferg's present overall state of mind anyway, remembering the effects, not all of which were visible, of the shootout the he'd endured those few months before. Crap in his drawers, now puke in his shoes. Guys have cracked for less. Like that very morning, when he, Sylvain Deacon, was ready to off two hounds.

In the alley Ferg's pant leg is still held high, fingers of the other hand waving the soiled paper bag and Sylvain Deacon while staring at the paper bag is suddenly nauseated himself and he will not talk for some time, not even to Lucille, about what happens next, being too embarrassed and not inclined to believe in out-of-body experiences and the like, but it happens though, that the spirit of Styler Ferguson seems for a moment to leave its body and enter that of Sylvain Deacon. There is no other explanation for the evil chill Sylvain suddenly feels, and a voice not his own that momentarily turns his world upside down as his own stomach does a cake-walk. I feel like Styler Ferguson, the voice says, and the bizarre—the voice continues—should be heavily documented just for verification of events like this. He envisions grabbing blindly for an oar, an oar that points down into the green porridge-like substance of the swamp (the swamp, a priest friend would later conclude, being

Sylvain Deacon's own unbelieving soul), then a barrage of images engulfs him, from the obscene to the mediocre, the one most vivid of a map of Canada on one's boyhood wall, all the rivers marked.

The experience had lasted only seconds but had left him shaken and now the dark of the gravel pit with a body lying at their feet does nothing to ease his already fragile nerves, perhaps a nagging doubt as to how much longer he can do this kind of work. Ferguson has removed his toes from the beam of light and is standing with shoulders slumped, his head at a thoughtful angle.

"You know Deac, I read in the paper the other day there was this kid. North Carolina or some place. Took this forty-five automatic to class one day. I think they were in the seventh grade about. Kids taking guns to school and killing their classmates is nothing new, I know, but these other kids give this kid the razz about something an' he opens up. Killed one of the little beggars and was responsible for one of the biggest laundry bills in the school's history. And they ask this kid why he did it. And you know why he did it? Know why he said he did it, Deac? Said because they bugged him all the time about being fat an' smart. Can you believe that?"

Sylvain Deacon stands long and lean against the night, the beam from the flashlight forming a tent of light over the John Doe and casting shadows across the irregular ground around the body and once more over the tips of Ferguson's shoes. Soon there would be more lights to help in the coming tedious search they both forebode, through the dead dark for clues, and most probably with dick-all results.

He waits but Ferguson says nothing, only the toes of his shoes can be heard rocking up and down in the tent of light, scrunching on the gravel. An occasional glint comes from the metal clasps on his belt.

"Well? What happened to the kid?" Sylvain finally says.

"The kid? Well, shit. He blew his brains out obviously. What the fuck would you do if you were fat an' smart?"

They're still in the pit, the mounds of gravel rising black around them, the occasional sound of the stones rolling down and shifting, like water running. Lights of the city reflect across the water, a thin ragged finger of the inlet that forms a small bay just east of the gravel pit. There's no wind here, just the sound of a tug chugging under the bridge. The beam of light from Sylvain's flashlight begins to tremble and then gyrate along the ground. Rodent-like sounds rise from his throat and Ferguson can be seen sinking slowly into a wobbly crouch down into the beam of light, his shoulders beginning to shake and with a hand raised to his forehead. And making the same sounds. The beam from the flashlight gyrates upwards, the original target forgotten, and shakes there all the harder disintegrating against the heavens.

"Jesus christ. Let's get back to the car!"

The beam of light plummets to the ground, lighting the way across the tire-torn shadows along the floor of the gravel pit. Styler Ferguson places a hand on the shoulder of Sylvain Deacon for support. Oh God, to just get in the car and close the doors. Check the police radio to make sure it's not sending. Then roll up the windows, hunch forward or lean back, and let the laughter come.

In this last act there is meant no lack of respect for the dead, either resting deep in the ground or lying stiff as a board above it. They know that occasional hysterics are passing and intrinsic—as the Chief in the past has so often opined to the media—to the nature of the work. And as for Sylvain Deacon, his forehead pressed against the backs of his hands that are gripped around the steering wheel, it's all the easier to appreciate the comedy. Although long and lean now, as a child he himself had been one of the fat and smart ones. Like the kid in North Carolina, getting the razz from the more athletic and thick-skulled of your classmates, and he too had wished the bastards six feet under.

He fights himself into control, swept with guilt pertaining to the dead in general. If he had to he could explain his and Ferg's behaviour and ask those offended to forgive the tactlessness, and explain that you had to be here. There is this body see, half sunk in the ground. A truck backed over it after its head was bashed in. There's only its arse gazing up at the stars, but you can easily imagine its front, facing Heaven's door and fumbling with the latch. And forty-fives popping off in classrooms, fat an' smart kids getting revenge, naked bodies perched and threatening on rooftops. And he would explain that it's only people that do these things, Nature has a dark side and it's us. We live funny and we die funny. What can you say?

He sits up, turning to Styler Ferguson. Concern replaces his guilt. Ferg appears to be laughing, still convulsed, but in mirth or pain? Maybe he hasn't really recovered from that shoot-out. Think about it. This may be the time for Ferg to crack, release the fetters, seek out the edge and over it go. At least he'd go nuts with a smile on his face. That same afternoon earlier, between the puke on Ferg's shoes and this lonely dark night yuk with the Pancake

Man, they'd been called to the Ho Inn Restaurant on Pender. A shooting between the Yellow Eagles and the Viet Chow, Asian youth gangs. And they had stepped carefully over another body then, this one shot once through the head. Complained about the food, Ferg had muttered, easing the tension and keeping himself from running screaming up the street. Sylvain identifies the smell of spring rolls and honey sauce. Two shots were fired and it's obvious where one has gone. He studies the wall—covered in a huge painting of a red and gold dragon—looking for the second bullet hole. Then—there!—through a weak spot in the wall behind the cashier counter where it continued into the Yen Sing Groceteria next door to lodge in another head, this one thankfully only of lettuce. While inspecting the hole, shouting erupts from the kitchen, he and Ferguson rushing in, new smells of spicy pork buns and spinach dumplings, Styler Ferguson sniffing and expertly singling out the egg soup with tomato. Two Chinese cooks are holding a gang member of the Viet Chow, one threatening him with a soup ladle and the other with a butcher knife. Sylvain decides to wade in, Ferguson hanging back, Sylvain looking like Gulliver midst the Lilliputians. The Viet Chow wrestles free and dashes off, Ferguson receiving an unintended blow across the forehead from the soup ladle in the confusion. Sylvain giving chase after the Viet Chow, finding himself battling his way through a hanging maze of chrome and steel, wangs and bangs of pots and woks heard on his passing head and arms. An ominous vat of wonton is overturned on the way, hissing waters underfoot as he fights for balance and flies on. Voice of the Viet Chow crying out ahead, hand accidentally dipped in the deep fryer. He ducks a skillet thrown by the Viet Chow as Ferguson is seen coming from the other side of a mile-long chopping table, a bowl of rice congee with liver airborne into the hanging pots and pans from where Ferguson's elbow has made contact with it. More wangs and bangs of woks and pots, the feet of the Viet Chow seen skidding unchecked through spilled dry-cooked beans toward the oncoming arms of Styler Ferguson, Ferguson with a face of fury now enlivened with rice congee and a soup ladle welt as a vast wok of *hor fun* noodles and a toppled tray of minced pigeon greets both. Styler Ferguson is first on his feet, buffeting the head of the Viet Chow, Sylvain spying a superlative cut of honey-baked ham steaming on the chopping block as he catches up and, with mouth watering, pulls Ferguson off.

And that had been their afternoon, Styler Ferguson standing out on the street covered in noodles and minced pigeon, restaurant patrons and management in hysterics, Ferg happy only because every other poor bugger, for once, seemed to be doing the screaming, shouting about the injustice of it all.

From the squad car in the gravel pit they squint into the glare. Shafts of light from headlights bounce off the dark mounds of gravel, rippling in a frenzy of jagged flashes across the tire-ridged ground.

"Here come the cops!" coughs Styler Ferguson, not trying to be funny. He drags a shirt sleeve across his face to clear the tears.

Vehicles are pulling into the pit, Sylvain Deacon's concern for Ferguson turns to alarm, alarm not for Ferguson but for the dead stiff. One of these assholes is sure to run over the already run-over body. He leaps from the car hoofing it over to the half-submerged corpse, waving his flashlight. Don't park here you assholes, he's had enough. Good christ—two ambulances, five squad cars, a forensics van, three unmarked vehicles and a fire truck. Fire truck? We've quit laughing guys, why can't you. Jesus, maybe the ladder will afford a better view for god's sake. Can get some good composite shots from above the Pancake Man, to show maybe to Mrs. Pancake.

The sudden activity seems incongruous to the up-till-now still of the gravel pit. He feels momentarily disoriented and pauses to catch his breath. Looks down at the Pancake Man, once walking around upright, maybe only hours before, possibly looking up at the sky and contemplating how to spend his RSP or coming vacations. Once staring out at the world and now staring down into it.

Floodlights are positioned, lighting up the area. Radios crackle and yellow tape appears. Styler Ferguson hangs back by the car safely out of the light, afraid of being delivered a quiet order by someone in authority to search the area, in the dark, maybe for hours, looking for God knows what and finding at most a crumpled cigarette pack, some empty gin bottles, or a used condom.

He moves deeper into the shadows.

The car radio crackles and he pounds his fist on the roof of the car. Lord, what now. Now what, where, why, when—whatever.

He leans in the door, yanking the mike. He manages to speak soberly, listens to the call. Calls Sylvain Deacon over, then signals to him he won't be a minute. Sylvain Deacon watches as Ferguson makes for the now taped perimeter around the half-buried body. Ferguson stands there a minute looking over, then walks slowly back to the car occasionally looking back. He looks disappointed.

"What's up?"

"Nothing. Wondered if his eyes were still open."

Sylvain Deacon feels rankled, an uncomfortable rising in his guts. Things were getting downright ghoulish.

"Jesus."

"I don't know. Just curious, you know. They're gonna lift him out in a sec."

Sylvain Deacon climbs swiftly into the car—jesus christ! Jack-off in the mouth of a cobra, snuggle up to a six-inch Australian blue-ringed octopus that holds enough poison to kill ten men if you want kicks, but right now get into this car and let's just get the hell out of here. One needs a shower or something. Lock up your sons and daughters, people. Murder, rape and pillage are still the foremost attractions down here. And the eyes of dead men, open or closed, tell only one story, don't they? That, no, at this time one does not particularily want to die. Isn't that it?

He backs the car up—something there—a detective discovered bent over, looking for clues. And now sprawled on the ground by the rear bumper and shouting angry questions. Sylvain Deacon looking around out his window, unable to reply. Don't these bozos know what kind of day it's been? Get out of the way, asshole, we're leaving. Your questions are all good and need answering, but only after deep inner searching and a two-six of scotch. He turns to Ferg.

"What's the call, again?"

"Call?"

"Where we going!"

"Oh. Altercation at gas station, Second and Main. Some fracas goin' down. Fight or something. Not too clear."

"Terrific."

Styler Ferguson twists around, looking back at the field of lights.

"Well?" says Sylvain Deacon.

"What?"

"Are they open or closed?"

"Can't tell from here."

"Terrific."

The tires spray gravel onto Wylie Street, Styler Ferguson laying an elbow out the window as the siren comes alive. Sylvain Deacon stares ahead through the windshield. "An altercation at Second and Main," they say, and he can only pray it's nothing too serious or plain vile. And Styler Ferguson beside him prays too, that this long shift ends soon, and it's not trouble with those gooks again.

16

Life Gets Better

JERRY LOWE, AS HE WILL later attempt to explain, has not deserted Hector at the Shell station at Second and Main. He is, as Hector Lake lands his roundhouse on the head of one of the brown-faced guys, squeezed into the back of the rust-primered shitbox in an alleyway a block and a half away and bent out of shape almost as much as the bird cage which he is trying to remove from the space behind the back seat. He's turned the one working headlight off, but, as the rules of the shitbox dictate, has left the motor running. Never turn everything off, he'd long ago established, lest nothing ever starts again. And christ, don't this bird's eyes look like they're running on something too, turning red to yellow and back to red from the glow of a distant streetlight.

Jerry Lowe has never, in his recollection at least, run from any altercation. On the contrary, he has always run headlong toward them consumed for the most part with a mindless fury bordering on a death wish, heedless of consequence or the odds. It has meant many a beating, more losses than wins, and it's remarkable to him that he has even had the presence of mind to get the damning evidence of their earlier crime away from the centre of the action. He's changing, maybe becoming less reckless, action and reaction becoming tempered with, of all things, rational thought and a new sense of self-preservation.

He gathers himself, then yanks hard on the cage. Hector must have welded it in. And keep an eye on your fingers gripping the wire, this wacko bird would like nothing more than to rip them off. And please stop with the fucking screeching while you're at it, bird, it'll get you nowhere. The pride of the anglo world is this night at stake, back at the gas station lot. Burn one's feathered bridges, buddy, the old life is gone. Give up. One accepts when one's been had, on to a new life, be it a literal shot in the arm for one's friends. To be of service to someone in this world is one of life's highest achievements. Wear your plume with pride, you evil scum-sucking bastard, the pride of the anglos. And quiet down. Else someone is going to rip that plume right out of your freaking head.

He stands erect and panting outside the rust-primered shitbox, the twisted birdcage full of mad flapping and screeches clutched to his chest. Can feel his heart pounding—jesus—hide this thing so one can go back and save face. Go back and save Hector Moses.

Although he does fear for Hector—Hector is back there outnumbered three to one—he is consoled somewhat with the knowledge that Hector carries with him a streak of recklessness, even fearlessness, that far exceeds his own and may do him well in the present circumstances. Hector told him once about the Crash Box, a go-kart of sorts that he and his friends built when he was a kid in Santa Monica. It consisted of no more than a plywood box with a lid mounted on a wood frame, in turn mounted on four wheels. No window holes (that was part of the thrill), no steering mechanism; the frame was fixed. A few pillows were allowed to be crammed inside the box around the rider, the box being barely large enough to fit one scrunched-up body. A course was selected, a steep hill somewhere with some obstacle at the bottom, the best obstacle being a drop-off or dense trees. The rider was then stuffed inside and the lid closed and latched from the outside. The Crash Box was then pushed off to rocket down the slope, the best slopes being grassy or stony inclines to add to the turbulence of the ride. Hector had described the sensation, scrunched up in the dark, aware of bone-jarring movement but with no idea of how fast you're going or for how long. Time slowed down according to Hector, and the anticipation of the final crash when and if the Crash Box reached the chosen obstacle was a thrill, Hector had said, that he has often since tried, but failed, to duplicate.

He gets back to the task at hand, stumbling with the cage away from the car through some weeds and working the strategy through his mind. Best to get it somewhere off the beaten track. Stash it here, in these tall forlorn grasses alongside this crumbling building wall. Cover it over with this handy plank and a hunk of cardboard over here from B.C. Apples. An empty grocery bag and a discarded shirt with holes, down here among the ruins. And pile the shit high around it for sound-proofing and weigh it down with these discarded paint cans.

He finishes and goes back to the shitbox, climbing in. It's probably wiser to park it and go back to the gas station on foot. One less thing to have to worry about.

At the mouth of the alley is a vacant lot where he turns the shitbox in, cutting the motor. He starts back up the alley, hearing the muffled cries of the bird from its hiding place as he passes the spot. No one will hear, he reassures himself, it's an industrial area and deserted for the most part at night. Might as well shut up bird, Egyptians buried themselves to last thousands of years, you can last an hour. Life gets better, you'll see. Maybe they will save the whales and ban all nuclear weapons. And you're going to make some people very happy, the ultimate gift that one gives . . . whether—they—want—to—or—not.

17

Decent Citizens

STYLER FERGUSON SPIES THE SHELL SIGN FIRST, a few blocks ahead and revolving slowly atop a pole at the corner of the intersection of Second and Main. He cranes forward for a better look trying to see between the low flat forms of the surrounding warehouses and industrial buildings. It would be nice to have a little warning of what's coming.

"Don't see any trouble."

Sylvain Deacon turns off the siren, the only fun part of the evening. As for trouble, anyone knows that's something you never see. Ferg should know better.

"Ask not for whom the bell tolls, buddy," he says.

Styler Ferguson grunts, but immediately wonders: That mean somethin'?

They pull in under the lights, Sylvain Deacon not happy with what he sees. From the station building doorway a thin guy in coveralls seems to be playing peek-a-boo from the shadows. Under the revolving Shell sign three more guys are crouched at the side of a souped-up green Camaro and at the sight of the police car all three leap to their feet.

"Oh, boy . . ."

The three start shouting at once, arms windmilling above their heads.

"Oh, boy, oh dear boy . . ."

Styler Ferguson, knowing what the Deac means this time, looks away and up the street.

"Great. First the gooks and now the doos."

"Easy, Ferg, no need for that. I'll handle it."

Sylvain Deacon heaving himself out of the car, hands up adjusting his hat and then down adjusting his belt, around and tugging the fold of his trousers out of his arse. He walks over to the Camaro. Styler Ferguson climbs out too but stays watchful by the car, happy to let Deac make the first move.

Sylvain Deacon is watchful too, although in no way happy, as his eyes follow the fingers of the three guys pointing down to the side of the green Camaro. Rust-coloured flakes mix in a jagged scrape along the green. And under his shoes, a lazy crunch of broken glass.

At the sound of the crunching glass the fingers turn and start pointing at his feet. Then they point up at the sky. Then all the fingers point south, up along Main, and with each new direction pointed comes a renewed volley of complaints, most of them a mixture of English and something else.

He holds up his hands for silence.

Styler Ferguson watches from the open door of the cruiser. He sees the Asian guys pointing at the Camaro's door, then down at Deacon's feet, then just as quickly up to the sky, down again and up along Main. And this is good, another eyewitness report to make sense of. It appears something fell out of the sky. And then it kicked in the doos' door and headed up Main. These guys are obviously whacked out on some religious yoga-incense-mind-warp fucking thing. And from the sounds of it, no-speaka-the-English very good either. He does notice—but doesn't want to—the thin pair of coveralls out of the corner of his eye beginning to make their way over. And he notices too, not wanting this either, another pair of coveralls, wider, standing down at the far end of the carwash. These coveralls have their back turned, and from appearances, and against what you might expect, are soaking wet from the waist up.

He feels uneasy, a gut instinct. All is not altogether right here, even without the Pakis. And his suspicions aren't helped by seeing the thin pair of coveralls flick a glowing cigarette butt at the gas pumps as they approach, his eyes follow the glowing ember along a ball-tightening romp through some purple and green stains of gasoline.

He attempts a cool, what he'd call a who-fears-an-asshole expression, as the thin coveralls light another cigarette and stop beside him. Christ, no one ever wants to appear cowardly or weak-kneed but the things you got to do to be a man. He finds his eyes are forced to do the impossible, look two directions at once. Watch this guy and watch that cigarette. You never have enough eyes in the police business, he knows, or other organs for that matter. And the big muscle in the rear, not always dependable, to hold everything in.

He pulls out his notepad. It usually helps to at least look official.

"You the one who called?"

The head on top of the coveralls nods.

"Yeah. I work here. Assistant Manager."

"Name?"

"Conrad . . . Parker."

Styler Ferguson's pen scratches in the notepad. Parker, Conrad.

"And you're the Assistant Manager?"

"Yeah. I just said that—"

Ferguson throws him an evil look. His pen scratches again. Asst. Manager—Shell stn, 2nd & Main.

"So, what's the problem, Mr. Parker?"

"Well, I'm not sure exactly . . ."

And isn't that a big surprise, thinks Styler Ferguson.

"Well? What happened?"

The Assistant Manager hesitates. "These two cars pull in and everyone gets out and starts fighting—"

"What two cars?"

"Well, that Camaro there and another. An old Volkswagen bug. But it's gone now I guess."

Styler Ferguson looks around. "Yes, I guess it is." His pen scratches. VW—AWOL.

"And what about these other guys in the Volkswagen, Mr. Parker. What they look like?"

"Uh . . . two guys and a girl. White guys. The white guys started fighting those East Indian guys over there and the chick split up the street. I didn't know what was going on so I called you guys. When I come out the Volkswagen's gone and only the big white guy's left fighting the three of them." He points over to the Camaro. "Then the big white guy takes off and catches up with the girl. Bops one of those guys on the head and just takes off."

"They just walk off? You get a license number?"

"Yeah. No."

"Well, what did these guys do?" Styler Ferguson jabs his thumb at the green Camaro.

"Nothing." The coveralls shrug. "Oh, they yelled and stuff but they couldn't do much. That white guy was big."

Styler Ferguson scratches. No license #—S.F.A.

He turns away and sees Sylvain Deacon coming back as a second cigarette butt bounces off the gas pump opposite. His pen dances. Parker, Conrad—run check!

Sylvain Deacon stops by the car. Ferguson is in no mood to wait for a Deacon well-let's-see-pause-pause-fuck-around explanation.

"Well, Deac? What gives?"

"Not much. These guys are a little hysterical. I'd say they're a little drunk too. Say two white guys and a woman in an old Volkswagen rammed them, put that dent in the side. Seems then they got out and sparred off a minute. One of the Asian guys took a good whack and the white guys took off."

"They weren't so fucking dumb," says Styler Ferguson. "That's what I got from Mr. Parker here. He's the guy who called. Assistant Manager."

"Mr. Parker?" says Sylvain Deacon.

"Yeah. I called."

Sylvain Deacon nods, staring off up the street. Styler Ferguson looks over at the green Camaro.

"What kind of idiot would ram a hopped-up machine like that in a freaking Volkswagen?" He scratches at his pad. Hit & run—Camaro whacked / no injuries.

A cry goes up from the direction of the Camaro. The three of them, the Assistant Manager included, instinctively ducking their heads, the notepad and pen of Styler

Ferguson airborne as his hand once again that day fumbles for his revolver.

"Jesus mother christ, Deac! Now what?"

Sylvain Deacon turns and sees the three Asian guys shouting and pointing at a white guy emerging from the darkness of the alleyway behind the carwash.

"You want I should call the wagon?" sputters Styler Ferguson, fishing for his pen from under the car.

Sylvain Deacon straightens, cheeks ballooning with an expulsion of air.

"No. Just call Lucille, Mr. Ferguson. Tell her that after twenty years on the force I've never had to fire my gun. Until tonight."

Ferguson looks over to the green Camaro.

"Gonna fire it three times maybe, eh Deac?"

Sylvain Deacon shoves his finger into his mouth.

"Maybe just onoo, buddy."

He walks back to the Camaro. The white guy, fresh from the night's shadows and slightly winded, plants himself next to him, likely seeking some protection. Sylvain Deacon's features bear an almost solemn countenance, he stands with toes pointed out, soles of his shoes rocking back and forth on the crunchy glass. From back at the squad car Styler Ferguson sees him raise the palms of his hands once again, gesturing for silence. The phrase, "Bridging the gap between cultures," comes to his mind from a speech the Chief frequently gives to the press or anybody else that's after the Department over any on-again off-again racial issues. The Deac's voice comes to him loud and clear.

"OKAY! QUIET! ONE AT A GODDAMNED TIME OR I'LL LOCK YA ALL UP!"

Everybody shuts up. The hiss and hum of the carwash mingles with the hiss and hum of traffic passing along Main. The mouth of Sylvain Deacon is moving, Ferguson can see, some words to get by. It doesn't matter what he's saying. Just straighten these assholes out. And the goofball Assistant Manager is lighting yet another cigarette, but all-in-all it appears things may be winding down, barring an explosion of the entire lot.

But things wind up again almost immediately as a fresh barrage of shouts erupt from the three Asian guys. Styler Ferguson is able to understand only a part of it.

"*Haram da!*" "This is he!" "THAT'S HIM, MAN!" "*Trakka hoea haram da!*" "This is the bastard, *polis!*" "*Pharna eh kutta!*" "*Nashebaz! Nashebaz!*"

He takes a few steps, eyes falling for a moment on the newspaper that lays open on the front seat of the car. Of course, just beneath the story of a burning tanker off the coast of Newfoundland, the words: INDIA/UPI—Sikh Uprising Nears Total Rebellion. He knew he'd heard of this shit somewhere. And what's with the Deac, staring off into space when he should be telling those yahoos to cool it.

Sylvain Deacon is staring off into space, adrift in a mild state of catatonia, a solution of late whenever confronted by too much stress in a given situation. He can hear again some far away sea, yes, there it is. Like listening to a shell put up to your ear, like the revolving yellow scallop turning slowly on the pole above. Put that thing up to your ear and you'd be able to drown everything out. And he can envision waves, waves engulfing first the white sand then engulfing all, folding in terrible blue and cold white curls over green pastures, over farmers' fields and climbing rocky cliffs, rolling down grey sidewalks and whole cities suddenly submerged, one's pension seen floating by. And even now he can be sure the revolving yellow scallop above is saying something, yes, it's talking to Sylvain Deacon. Saying, Yak, Yak, Go Away. Go south. Enough is enough. Close eyes. Don't move or say anything. And get out of trouble. Any way you can.

Styler Ferguson has moved closer during this last outburst from the three Asian guys, ready to assist if they decide the white guy now standing beside Sylvain Deacon is to be castrated or otherwise mutilated to satisfy certain religious rites. While never obliged to openly admit of any hidden racist tendencies, he has seen these peoples' fat half-naked god, the Buddha or whatever, on postcards and in books, sitting cross-legged in parks and on piles of stone with thick-lidded eyes, snakes all over the place, and judging by some of its expressions, with a carrot up its ass. And who really knows what goes through these peoples' minds, weaned on all sorts of questionable and just plain weird voodoo temple stuff. They've got that Kama Sutra for god's sake, a religious fuck book, and a holy river that the whole country bathes and pisses in.

He stands, tensed for action. Sylvain Deacon seems to have snapped out of whatever stunned pie-eyed trance he was in and is saying something to the white guy. The white guy nods and begins to—walk away?

Styler Ferguson watches him go in disbelief, as do the three Asian guys, the white guy heading back up the alleyway next to the carwash. The three Asian guys really go crazy this time—and who can blame them—what the fuck was the Deac doing?

He scratches in his pad. S.D. lets guy go / S.F. not consulted.

Sylvain Deacon is making for the squad car, ignoring the commotion. Stops at the driver's side and pulls back a cuff at the end of a long arm to check his watch.

"It's that time, buddy. We're history."

Ferguson spiralling his hat into the back seat. "Right!"

They climb into the car, Sylvain Deacon wincing as he sits on his handcuffs. A volcanic roar comes from the green Camaro, the dark windows now rolled up. It pulls out onto the street in an exaggerated show of caution.

"Gee, Deac. Think that guy always drives like that?"

Sylvain Deacon snorts, busy with the radio to call in a brief report. Styler Ferguson is aware suddenly of the Assistant Manager, momentarily forgotten, still standing by the car and letting loose yet another glowing cigarette butt while his head keeps swiveling up and down Main Street.

"Think those guys are going to be mad I called the cops?" he says.

Styler Ferguson looks up at him from the police car window.

"Those guys?"

"Yeah. The white guys too."

"Uh . . . don't worry about them, buddy. If any of them come back, call us. We'll shoot 'em in the knee caps."

Conrad Parker attempts a nervous smile. Only an idiot would fall for this cop's bravado crap. But he doesn't move, standing in what looks to Styler Ferguson like expectation, a need for yet more reassurance.

Styler Ferguson reads the label on the thin coveralls.

"Uh. . . Conrad, is it? Well, Conrad. One more thing you

can do. I'd get that glass cleaned up before somebody drives in and blows a tire. Don't want to get shit for that too, eh?"

Conrad Parker's eyes dart to where the whisky bottle lays shattered across the pavement. And pulling in just then off Main Street, a camper truck, its tires crunching over the glass.

Good grief, thinks Styler Ferguson, let's finish this up!

"Yeah, okay, Conrad. And thanks for calling in." He rolls up his window. That's enough encouragement and kind words for Joe Public. It's probably more to his advantage now to give some words of encouragement to Sylvain-Fucking-Deacon, who seems, goddamnit, to be sitting waiting for something.

"Let's go, Deac!"

A baseball cap sticks itself out the window of the camper.

"Officer!"

Styler Ferguson leaves his window rolled up.

"Officer! Trouble on the road only a short time ago. Thought it our duty to report as decent citizens, believers in the Almighty, as I suspect you are too, sir. The trauma struck to the heart of mother here, put her off her McDonalds—"

"Deac!"

Sylvain Deacon sets the car in motion, the wheels crunching over the broken glass. They pull onto Main, Styler Ferguson deciding to holler an excuse out the window to the baseball cap still seen sticking out the window of the camper. "Sorry, sir. Have a call! Police emergency!" And in the rearview mirror a colour postcard of the Assistant Manager standing under the brightly lit canopy, ignoring the guy in the camper truck and watching them go.

"Oh, jesus, Deac, I'll tell you. That's one lonely blowjob back there, man. Or something. That bastard's gonna blow himself to shit one of these days. I'll bet on it."

Sylvain Deacon cracks his elbows.

"Yes. Kind of a lost soul that one, Mr. Ferguson."

"Lost? That poor guy's gone. There's no finding people like that."

Ferguson leans back, stretching an arm along the seat. "Okay, Mr. Deacon. So what the hell happened?"

Sylvain Deacon drives slowly, at this time of your day an experienced cop wants to keep his eyes directly ahead, see no evil. Time to let the goons out there go at each other if they want to. You've done your shift. Now just dump the car, report in, and get home.

"Well, Deac?"

"Well, nothing. Really. We reached . . . an understanding. I told the white guy it would be better if he just went home."

"Went home?" Jesus christ, thinks Styler Ferguson. "Went home for god's sake," he continues. "Was he one of the other guys or not?"

"Yeah, he was one of the other guys."

"And you told him to go home . . ."

"He asked if I'd seen the other two. The big guy and the girl. I said they'd headed up the street."

"You said they'd headed up the street . . ."

"Uh huh."

"And then you said it'd be better if he just went home . . ."

"Right."

"And he went . . ."

Jesus christ, thinks Sylvain Deacon.

Ferguson, almost shouting: "WELL, DID HE RAM THE DOOS' CAR OR NOT?"

"With what?"

Styler Ferguson looks over, laughs. "No wonder the doos were pissed."

"Well, what can you do? The white guy was just standing there. Those Asian guys were half cut anyway and were getting on my nerves. Not even speaking English half the time."

Styler Ferguson feels he deserves the laugh, a little something back for a hellish day.

"You didn't run those guys through the database? Did you get their names even?"

"Entered their licence plate number. Should be enough if there's more trouble."

"Let me tell you just how screwed up the world is Deac. There's some black guy over in Africa at the moment calling himself the 'Emperor' of Africa. I read it in the paper. This guy is accused, get this, among other things, of eating people."

Sylvain Deacon watches the road ahead, smiling at an image of a candlelit table somewhere, chandelier hanging above and on a plate of fine English bone china, a human leg in honey sauce.

"And get this, Deac. His cook or servant or some fucking thing says he gets them cooked up and served. The whole bit. He's got this walk-in freezer with the bodies hanging. Now picture that for your raving nutcase. Says he likes to 'eat his political enemies.' I mean, for fuck's sake. A dipshit world."

For the second time that night Sylvain Deacon begins to emit tiny rodent-like sounds.

"Sometimes I think we could use someone like that in Ottawa—hey, Deac—you okay?"

And under the moon, still above somewhere in its perigee, a police blue-and-white, emergency lights in shadow, pulls itself over to the curb while inside one head flops forward on the steering wheel as a second head falls back on the seat, the mouth of one open wide to the ceiling, to the stars, images of Bosch and Van Gogh, centuries of madmen and artists inbred in the boonies, deformed heads the size of ash cans, as the car fills, swarms, with raucous screeching and upward inflections, but this time not from a bird, but from another day done over in what Sylvain Deacon has to agree with his partner, seems at best none other than a dipshit world.

18

Sweet Humming Motors

SINGH SIDHU BLINKS, HEARING HIS NAME. The inky shadow oozes over his legs once again. Looking down at him, the concerned face of *sajjan* Jagit. He rubs his head, wishes to speak but cannot—would like to give the boys a mantra. Something gained from all this sitting on one's arse on the pavement. "And what, dear *sajjania*, is the sound of one bunghole a-landing?"

A police blue-and-white has turned into the lot, the siren cut short where a moment ago it howled, the last note lingering in Singh Sidhu's ears, still ringing, still there, but there is something else. Something lost, perhaps. Unfinished. Some treasured personal article dropped into a deep mucilaginous bog which you'll never see again . . .

A tall cop with silver hair is asking questions of Jagit Sanghera and the brother younger and their voices rise and fall with replies, moving left and right, up and down, oblong circlings of English and Hindi as Singh Sidhu hears his own voice join in. Be accurate and tell all. One may still receive justice.

But with telling all, doubt begins to creep, like a rat

returning to a sinking ship, doubt over the possible difficulties explaining just exactly what has happened. About the rust-primered VW and the two white scuzbags who are nowhere in sight. Or the rust-primered Volkswagen either for that matter. And the caged white kid in the back seat, the disappeared white woman and all the evidence, thinks Singh Sidhu, no longer evident.

The tall cop is jotting down names. Yes, yes, *sajjania*, Singh urges inwardly, this is good. Give that cop answers to questions. Speak freely if not all at once, truckloads of objective impartial facts. They did it. The fucking white guys. Rammed the immaculate Green Behemoth. And what does the cop need our names for? Our license plate number?

Jagit Sanghera is pointing to the scraped side of the Green Behemoth but the cop doesn't seem to notice. Singh Sidhu feels a new irritation to add to the throb in his head and the throb along his tailbone. What more does this cop want? And now the fucker's walking away to talk with his partner who waits by the unpolicing police car. A chance, at any rate, to rub head and arse, one hand up, the other down. See if he can do both simultaneously, different directions. A good test for the motor reflexes and pray the old bunghole has not somehow, like some Egyptian tomb, been sealed forever.

He jumps.

Jagit Sanghera and the brother younger are shouting again, pointing to the alleyway behind the carwash. The white not-as-big driver guy has come out of the shadows, Singh Sidhu still rubbing head and arse. He can sense the white guy's surprise which resembles his own—put your nose up, buddy—sniff, sniff—there's trouble here in the air for you tonight.

The long lean cop returns threatening to lock them all up if they don't shut up. Then the long lean cop says nothing, looking up at the revolving yellow scallop, a finger in his ear. Singh Sidhu stops rubbing. The cop starts, like someone just nudged him, and says something to the scuzbag white guy driver who nods and walks away. Singh Sidhu's mind truely wavers, in every sense of the word. Somewhere between the Here and the There, the rap on the head and the rap they seem to be taking now. The white guy scuzbag is indeed going free, back up the alleyway from whence he came.

He winces, bolts of pain charging through his extremities. Do not tighten aching bunghole to express rage—safer to clench teeth instead. Or make fists.

Jagit Sanghera and the brother younger seem to be taking somebody's advice and are climbing into the Green Behemoth. Singh Sidhu follows, managing himself into the driver's seat.

"You okay to drive, Singh?" asks Jagit Sanghera.

"Yeah, but what the fuck's happening?"

"Just drive," says Jagit Sanghera. "Circle around."

Singh Sidhu complies, too tired to argue. He drives slowly out of the lot and turns right onto Second. A moment later Jagit says, "Turn down here."

Singh turns down and they cross some tracks, then he gets the idea. This road is bound to intersect the alleyway the scuzbag white guy was last seen walking down. He can feel the presence of Jagit Sanghera beside him, the brother younger in the back seat behind. His mind clears. He can feel the rumble of the Green Behemoth, the rumble of their breathing. The rumble of the floor panels and doors, the rumble of these three hearts of these three desperados. Six black eyes staring out on the night and looking for reptilian white guy slime-dogs or humped forms of rust-primered VW bugs.

"There it is!"

The brother younger is the first to spot the black hump sitting alone in a vacant lumberyard lot.

"And there *he* is," whispers Jagit Sanghera.

At the side of the humped shadow is a darker thinner one, hunched at the door. Singh Sidhu wheeling the behemoth into the lot, letting the beams from the headlights illuminate the battered Volkswagen. He tenses with excitement, then with pain.

Do Not Tense Bunghole.

Jerry Lowe has hurried back along the alley from the gas station. Things were working out—oh, cops and robbers, thugs and thieves, liars, pricks and general arseholes. And the freaking moon too. He's kept his freedom after all. It hadn't looked good when first walking out under the lights of the gas station and seeing no sign of Hector Lake or Katrinna. But one had to ditch that loony bird and get the shitbox out of the way. Then rush back to help Hector Lake only to find the Asian hordes going apeshit in the face of that beanpole copman. And who can believe it, the cop telling him to go. Had leaned over and said, "Maybe you just ought to go home." Had heard a creak from the revolving yellow scallop just at that moment, as if it too was giving the okay. Boss Gods in heaven, bless all tight-assed thugs and tortfeasors. One never knows, does one? It would seem at times that existence is nothing more than the series of unguessed seconds when predicaments change, not the months and years between.

He reaches the end of the alley and crosses the railroad tracks. Somewhere the rust-primered shitbox waits in the shadows, alone and patient under an all-knowing, and, now, forgiving night sky. To just start up that sweet humming motor, that one last fearsome hurdle, and pick up the loony bird where hidden.

Groping his way, streetlights are sparse. Cut through this darkened walkway between these two buildings. Watch the ditch, dark as a rat's ass down there. Things heard scrambling away in the black. Jesus. The huge mirrored Expo Golfball seen glowing from across this bit of harbour, the city skyline beyond lit like a christmas tree. A whole city lit up and one can't even find a rust-primered shitbox. He isn't keeping enough mental notes of what he's supposed to be doing. Used to keep lists all the time: Do laundry, pay the bills, scrape the green stuff off the fridge door. Now he just leaves it all to fate, hoping he'll figure it out as he goes along.

A turn here, not familiar. Up ahead a high fence and black building shapes. A wasteland of warehouses and industrial sites where no one lives, a deserted ruin within the city. A black hump, the black hump of a rust-primered shitbox if ever there was one, still distinquishable even in the dark and still parked where he left it. And here comes the moon, out from behind the clouds to shine down, now when it's no longer needed, one complimentary beam. Thanks a lot buddy.

He fumbles with his keys.

Yeow, but is it dark. The world swallowed up. And what is the moon doing up there, gone again, shine your everloving light on me. This key to the house front door. This one to the back. Maybe. This other one the mail key, or this one. Christ, keys here to nowhere, everywhere. But bless the car-making Huns in Europe that the keys to Volkswagens, like the cars themselves, have their own distinct shape.

He fights control of his fingers, must be more shaken by the evening's events than had thought. Somehow to insert this key into its loving hole. Come on, baby. Slide inside. Got to fire up that motor, that last fearsome hurdle, and secure the bird. Go home and bolt the fucking door.

But, shit.

And shit again.

This key to keyhole, asshole. Have done it a thousand times, do it once more. Panic setting in, got to maintain calm. List one's observations: giddyness, anxiety, mind and body half here, half there. A life lived in fear, this will do it to you. A wise thing would be to cut down on boozatanical intakings, sometime soon, work toward some stability in his life for the world swings a mean bat at the heads of the unwary. And, christ, what's with the homespun homilies—philosophizing, if nothing else, is a sure sign of fear.

Now on his knees, nose to door, eye to keyhole. Now scraping, clawing, and hears the rumble. From behind—from above—one hopes not from below. Crouched at the side of the rust-primered shitbox and suddenly bathed in light. This can't be a blessing, some celestial message. Even the light of the gods comes from above, or at most, from within. Not straight into one's eyeballs across unlit vacant lumberyard lots. Not from rumbling green Camaros.

19

Western Gods Reign Supreme

JAGIT SANGHERA IS THE STOCKIER SHADOW out of the car, the brother younger a thinner shadow behind. Singh Sidhu climbs out the other side slowly, controlling muscle parts. The lot is enclosed by chain-link fencing, there's no need to hurry. The white guy scuzbag isn't going anywhere. But he sees the white guy scuzbag *is* going somewhere, even if it seems only in circles. He's moved around to the front of the VW where he lifts the hood and reaches in, his hand coming out holding a large black cross that he brandishes in the glare of the Behemoth's headlights. Singh Sidhu feels his elation drop, a religious fucking lunatic is all they need right now.

The black cross passes once more through the glare of the behemoth's headlights, two tubes joined at the middles, their ends shaped for wheel nuts. His elation rises again, it's only a make-shift weapon, not some mystical icon.

The white guy's stopped moving, squinting into the light. He's weighing the odds, thinks Singh Sidhu, and although white guy scuzbags may be inferior at most things, they can be pretty good with numbers. Three on one. And one Green

Behemoth against one rust-primered shitbox. Better run, dildo.

No sooner does he say this to himself than he sees the dildo does run, legging it along the ten-foot chain-link fence, topped, as Singh Sidhu now notices, with barbed wire. This is good, another odd in their favour.

Jagit Sanghera and the brother younger are already giving chase.

"Ha!" shouts Jagit Sanghera.

"You're dead, mother!" shouts the brother younger.

"Got you now, you—" Singh Sidhu doesn't finish, extremities once again zapped with bolts of pain. He hobbles after along the fence, peering ahead at the running shadows.

When Jerry Lowe is blinded by the glare of headlights, it interrupts his singing—*I don't care if it rains or freezes*—and mistakes, he thinks, are things ordered up in the past to be paid for in the present. And he's made a big one here by coming directly to the shitbox and not laying low for a while. An idea, extant from a hazy philosophy class long ago makes itself known: "Systematic thinking is of comparatively late development in human experience and even today, the experts say, the number of people that really control and order thoughts make for but a small minority of all mankind." And I'm here to prove it, he thinks.

Car doors can be heard opening somewhere from behind the glare, and christ, just for a moment one could swear the grillwork on that green beast is grinning. He moves, getting himself quickly around to the trunk of the shitbox. Lift the hatch, pull out this tire iron and brandish menacingly, the tire iron cross-shaped, three-pronged. Fake confidence, better still, madness, maybe these dinkshits are vampires and will shy away. Stranger things have happened this day, like stealing cockatoos. And where have gone the days when all one needed was a spear and a good stone to throw?

He crouches, then begins to skulk. Then straightens, ready to run. Keep up deceptive behaviour, can't see a thing. But the Asian hordes are there, behind the headlights. They seem confused. An inner debate on whether he should make a stand, let the end try the man. Got to stop with the quotes, a sure sign that fear is taking over. And keep brandishing the tire iron, may get at least one of these flibbertigibbets.

He takes a few steps away from the light, shaken by this last word that has come to mind. Got to hold on, these ghosts that won't die of a higher education. Can try to meet one's end sane and simple-minded at least. And there, behind the headlights, three gangly shadows.

Backing up, a jagged corner of the rust-primered shitbox rubbing his leg. Feels like it's tugging, holding on. Don't leave me. A glance down at the rust-primered shitbox and all its deformities, so much less to lose than it's owner. *May the gods be with you shitbox, one bears you company no more.*

One more quote and with iron cross in hand he's legging it along the ten-foot high chain-link fence. One has at least a lead off, the Asian hordes caught napping. And looking up with one's stomach tightening to see barbed wire running along the top of the fence at the same speed one is running below. From behind somewhere, but close, the clippety-clop of two or three pairs of sleazy boots giving chase, Jerry Lowe in full stride along the fence over the vacant lumberyard lot. The city skyline jiggling along in the corner of one eye, in the corner of the other, unrelenting curls of barbed wire and that eye told to look for a break. One could use a third eye, to see what's ahead. The fenced-in corner of the lot looming up, sealing off escape. *Abandon all hope ye who enter here*, let go another quote from somewhere. No matter, they won't want the intellect, and one is already deciding what to do when captured. Which body parts to protect, which to give up.

The fence ahead is backlit from the lights of Main Street, making a criss-cross pattern. And who needs the moon now, a concessional beam now and then, when one can see quite clearly the dead end that one is fast running into. There should be a quote or two for this but none come, just childhood images of heroic last stands—Indians painted with red and yellow stripes, Randolph Scott and Slim Pickins holding them off. And for the second time today one could again use a stand-in, someone to deliver choreographed blows on the enemy closing the gap behind. Out of quotes and images; one last look along that barbed wire, hope or luck or who gives a fuck. Don't believe what you think you see, a trick mirage induced by desperation and moon perigees, but the last few feet of fence top do seem free of barbed wire.

He keeps his pace, daring to hope. It can only be a hallucination brought on by fatigue and fear, boozatanical intakings. But climb the fence anyway, ignore the inevitable hack-job on one's face from the barbed wire you know is there. May buy some pity later from Katrinna Reticuli and Hector Lake.

Iron cross sailing over the fence, then wire links singing as he climbs. *As long as I got my plastic Jesus* . . . yeah, hum a few bars and keep your eyes shut. Some sparse protection from those prickly barbs one knows are still there. But, jesus, awful, felt falling into one's pants, an accident of Nature and a steamy voidance uncontrollably let go with the exertion of climbing. And no time to reflect on the morals and sanitary habits one struggles to live by, not even time to wrinkle one's nose.

He touches down on the other side, eyes open again and staring back through the wire mesh at two bodies climbing up in pursuit. A temptation to heckle, wiggle one's thumbs in one's ears, stick out his tongue. But this isn't the playground of one's childhood, things have escalated to real serious shit. These guys want blood, or worse, and best to pick up the iron cross and keep going.

To Singh Sidhu the late night regatta seems a pretty even race, the three others in front, their boots pounding along the base of the fence and nobody gaining or losing ground. He labours on bringing up the rear, a wince when the left foot comes down, a sigh for the right. Up ahead they're fast approaching the end of the yard—"The end of the line," he smiles. He's the slowest but now the most dangerous, caught up in the fever of the chase, the thrill of the kill. Through pain and suffering one's mind is not made free, he thinks, it simply goes. The fast fleeing shadow of the white guy scuzbag has somehow taken the form of his own shadowy fast approaching pre-arranged marriage, this making it all the more imperative to corner it and secure at least a symbolic annulment by pounding it senseless.

But this is the Western world and Western gods reign supreme, he knows, and can already see that the last few feet of fencing is not topped with barbed wire. And this is something Third World countries would do, for christ's sake, start something and not finish it.

He can see the white guy scuzbag doesn't even break stride, first lofting the tire iron over the fence and then up and over himself, the chain-links singing as he climbs. A clang as the tire iron lands. Then the scuzbag's down the other side, his shadow stooping to retrieve the iron and then disappearing into the night.

Jagit Sanghera and the brother younger attempt to climb after, the tips of their fingers grappling with the wire links, and through tear-streamed eyes Singh Sidhu sees it all from a half-lap behind, a few pathetic obscenities wheezing up from a gasping burning throat. But the white guy reappears for an instant, materializing out of the darkness on the other side of the fence but a few feet from where Singh now leans against it. Their eyes meet, a fraction of an instant, and Singh Sidhu sees not fear in the white guy scuzbag's eyes, but something more akin to wonder, a questioning of his present predicament, perhaps, a conclusion of some kind dawning while turning and disappearing once again into the shadows.

Clench only teeth and fists, he tells himself. And the white guy scuzbag is gone, an ill omen. Jagit and the brother younger stop climbing as imminent on the horizon lie marriage plans that are not gone, they're still on in fact, and this clinches it. The Green Behemoth took a beating in the side, Singh Sidhu in the head and arse. Karma. That's what this is. "Karma," the old man always says just before lowering the boom on you for something. Some kind of divine retribution for past lives and the evils you did. But one's past lives could never have been like this, life alone in a mountain cave contemplating the universe sounds good. Eating bats. Licking moisture from the walls. And it seems for the moment that one will never again take anything for granted, be happy, or shit without pain. He experiences then a great emptiness, perhaps this is what is meant as a state of non-being. And attained at so young an age, his father would be proud. Leaning against the fence, out of breath, out of hope. He thinks he feels a drop of rain—bring on the flood waters—karma coming down, karma coming down under the moon . . . bright eye of night . . . white sun, do your motherfucking worst.

20

Feast of All Souls

JERRY LOWE IS AS SURPRISED AS Singh Sidhu when they come face to face for that moment on opposite sides of the chain-link fence. He'd been dodging in and out of storage containers in the dark, trying to backtrack, not sure if the two brown-faced guys behind him had cleared the fence or not and were still giving chase. He pulls up for an instant, his eyes connecting with those of the third brown-faced guy leaning gasping against the fence. The guy looks in pain and his eyes look like those of the pursued instead of the pursuer. Jerry Lowe knows that look, has seen it in the mirror many mornings, especially lately. He feels no animosity, more like kinship, for the brown-faced guy appears to be just as lost as he is.

He turns back, away from the fence, finding himself wishing the poor guy well with whatever problems he's having. In the First and Second World Wars the opposing forces sometimes declared a short armistice and came out of the trenches to exchange greetings and the madness of what they were doing must have become apparent upon finding the enemy to be just like you, and just as baffled.

He stays low, sprinting bow-legged into the shadows, uncomfortably aware of the accident filling his pants. Rounding a corner and ahead a darkened shape—god knows—see if it's moving as one refuses to slacken speed. Not sure if those guys cleared the fence and could be anywhere setting traps. Keep an eye for trip wires, covered pits lined with spikes.

The darkened shape ahead closer now, an industrial waste container, lid up, black mouth to the black sky. And where one is headed. Out of one rust-primered *Narrenschiff* and about to leap into another, making like the hunchback Quasimodo across this open space, the hump on one's back now fallen into one's pants. Gather speed, as much as is possible in this position, Boy Scouts' motto of look before you leap unheeded and with wings borne of the gulls that circle garbage dumps daily, launch one's body high into the night air through which a light drizzle has begun to fall. A graceful arc born of fear, the world spinning by, the Expo Golfball seen rolling away to the right on a drive down an unlit fairway while coming down on one's back with a crunch on a bed of unknown things.

He lies unmoving in the waste container, face to the sky.

Feel about for shards of glass or metal things sticking through flesh, the Haitian Feast of All Souls now to begin. Can hear the living bodies of those now risen from the dead climbing the fence. The women will be decked in colourful shawls and straw hats; the men in white, faces solemn and grim. To come here and drop wine and bread over the side of one's crypt, food and drink for the lost soul of this dead family member now buried here. Oh, the sweet caring of other cultures, why was one born a honky?

He jerks, drop of rain right in the eyeball, another storm a-brewing. And with this another frightening thought—christ—do Hindus burn their dead? Or their enemies? Is it drops of rain one now feels or gasoline, a photo remembered from the paper glimpsed earlier today with the caption: Militant Sikhs In Golden Temple Protest, and a face, none too friendly, looking out from under an oily turban, an AK-47 cradled across a shoulder.

He lies quiet, hands out to the sides gripping unseen matter that feels like small sticks and mashed cardboard. And what the hell was he doing, anyway? Those brown-faced guys could be anybody. Members of the Khalistan Commando Force, or worse, the Bhindranwale, responsible for most of the terrorist acts in the Punjab, the article said. They're fanatics, while he, Jerry Lowe, was only unhappy. One still has the iron cross, it may well be needed. To stave in turbaned heads. To fix four flats on a rust-primered shitbox. Grandpa once described a similar situation, his body too lying in the muck of his brothers, a hole in France in 1918 likewise full of garbage and rot and he menaced by a different horde. Things don't seem to change that much and Grandpa claimed he'd learned something from all that but what was it? And are these East Indian guys really bad or just pissed-off because of the car? And Mom's latest letter says she wants to give away one's sporting equipment and Dad's drinking heavily, a beanpole cop stares up at a revolving scallop with his finger in his ear while Hector Moses swings a whisky bottle at the stars . . . and don't forget the bird—jesus—don't forget the fucking bird.

He dozes, or thinks he does. How long has he been lying here, waiting for three brown faces, maybe more, to appear over the top of these garbage container walls, night terror from the Punjab? Time now to sit up, look around. Vampires fear the light as hopefully do berserk Asian terrorist gangs. A faint glow now rising in the East, it's their sun too. Haven't had a quote in some time, one must no longer be afraid. Best to think no more of what is no more, surely the terrorists have all gone home. And Katrinna and Hector Moses are home now too, safe but not sound, junk-sick and full of worry. Raise up—ow!—something sharp there. Damp wicked smell too, humorous image of man in trash can, banana peel on head. Ha. Ha. No time for the funny stuff. Squish of something momentarily forgotten and gone cold in one's drawers, must fight the self-loathing, shake a leg, then the other. What better place to empty one's pants of fecal outpourings. And don't feel too bad, Grandpa suffered the same fate many times in the mud-filled trenches of 1918, shitting himself and rinsing off in the blood of dead rats. Or so the old bastard used to say.

Raising his head higher, look both ways before crossing early morning vacant industrial lots while climbing stiffly over the sides of waste containers. Feet touching down, slight trembling in the legs. Move quickly to cover, by a good solid wall. Could stop a slug from an AK-47. Inch head around the corner of this building, passed on the run an unknown time ago. Cross of iron at the ready, who or what do Sikhs worship, anyway? And thank one's own gods for a sudden inspiration—rip one's shirt so and wrap around head. Looks like a turban in this dim light, they'll think you're one of them. And see down at the far end of the madly run fence the humped shape of the rust-primered shitbox still parked there on the other side in the lumberyard lot, the first light of morning along its back in a sublime marriage of pink and gold. One can see beauty in anything at a time like this.

Another check and no sign of the green Camaro. But dogs are known to drop dead of starvation waiting for their masters to return. What of the patience of the Asian peoples? One has no choice, really, a whacked-out bird waits nearby, maybe even dead by now but if alive worth much to Katrinna Reticuli and Hector Moses. Drag one's weary body once again over this fence, *a stout heart crushes ill luck*. Another quote, fear must be returning. And one more cold turd falling from one's pantleg. So much the better.

Approaching along the fence towards the rust-primered shitbox, parts of shirt wound around his head. And relieved to see the tires have not been flattened. Some other dirty work done, the one working headlight now smashed in. The one working tail light smashed too, thought it was only the Muslims that put out the eyes. The rear window is no more, beads of shattered glass in a dull white mosaic covering the back seat. Around to the rear and raising the hood cover, expecting an empty compartment but the tiny motor still there staring back with all its parts. Miracles on miracles, a few more dents and bruises but who can tell? And one last spoiling, the radio antenna, of no use anyway, twisted into an expressionistic art piece.

Stiffly into the driver's seat, a grimace when sitting on one's trousers. The sky now streaked with pink, sunlight catching some early gulls soaring above. And pumping the steel rod where the gas pedal should be and turning the key, jaw clenched, this is the moment. The tiny motor back there under the hood with a yin-yin, yang-yang. A leap of the heart and tears almost to the eye as it springs to life, Jerry Lowe looking up through the ceiling thanking all the fairy godmothers, the Boss Gods in Heaven, one's lucky stars. Life thus sinks and rises grand. Living in the eye of the storm is surely worth the setbacks if only for these moments of reprieve and uplift.

He backs out—"Out of the frying pan, into the fire, and back again . . ."

A gull swoops low, skirts the fence, dips its wing in salute. If the world had balls, he thinks, I'd have it by them.

He crosses the stream soaking his feet and not caring, hellbent down the road. The grouse will be retrieved with the help of two buddies and a dog. One of the buddies, Bobby, will have nerve enough to forage for it at the base of the tree and drag it out by its neck which is broken, either by the pellet or the fall. They will even pluck it and eat it, his mother roasting it up. But he will never feel fully proud of the hunt. It was a fluke. The smaller brown balls were chicks, now orphans. And the point of it all will be lost on youthful concerns of what's cool and what isn't, or what matters and what doesn't. He will carry the rifle out on other excursions but never kill anything until it's finally confiscated by the police on a clear summer day a year later, not really missed that much by the now thirteen-year-old Jerry Lowe, who wanders unarmed down to the stream, stands in it in his sneakers and watches water bubble over them, scooping water spiders into his hands.

The Exaltation of the Heroes

21

Mad Is Bad, Again

UNDER THE WEAK GLOW from a distant streetlight chubby fingers tap the wire mesh. A black beak chomps a piece of baloney sandwich as a voice, like humming, pours forth.
 —Hey, birdie. This bird cage don't look so good. So bent. Who did this? Got run over maybe, fell off a truck. Hey, birdie. Where you come from? What you doing here? Heard you making noise and found you here under all this stuff. Always walk this way home though Momma says to stay out of the alleys. Use the main roads. Better light there. Take more baloney sandwich, birdie. No mustard. Scraped it off so it won't burn your tongue. Birds got tongues? I don't know. But someone does know these things, don't worry. Will be in a book somewhere. Someone knows everything. Not me, just Luther the retard. Almost got it good today, head in the carwash. Dangerous job but everyone think it's easy. Not for a retard. Nothing easy for a retard. Momma says different but I know. All hard, anything. Even talking, birdie, but I can. Can even swear if I want to. I know those words. Just like Mr. Conrad. I don't like it. Those words. No fun. I had beer tonight, birdie. It came in

a taxi car after the police went away. Gotta be careful. Just one from Mr. Conrad. Might make me crazy Mr. Conrad says. That's what it does. They say that. The ones who drink it. Like those people who come in tonight, couldn't see too well, birdie. Had soap in my eyes and got bonked good. But the best part comin', birdie. The policeman car with blue and red lights, like Playland. Everything turning, including Luther. Something got broken, birdie. Heard it smash. It's good Mr. Conrad has a party sometimes at the gas station. Otherwise he gets so sad. So mad. Mad is bad, birdie. Really. Luther got mad once, birdie, at Nurse. Being mean to Mr. Skinner at the hospital place. Said he couldn't crawl around on visitor's day. She didn't know, birdie. She didn't know Mr. Skinner he only crawl around on visitor's day. He doesn't walk. Too normal he says. That's how he gets his cigarettes. The people give them to him so he'll go away. It's a good joke, birdie. You would've laughed. One day I did it. For Mr. Skinner. He was sick. I got him eleven cigarettes, birdie. Mr. Skinner called me his good lad. Got a cigarette here, Mr. Conrad gave it to me too. Why Mr. Conrad give me all these things I don't know. Can smoke it. Wanna see. Birdies don't smoke, good idea. Bad up there to fly smoking. Eat your sandwich, got some more. Momma made 'em. Baloney and tuna fish, for Luther. I like that. But I don't eat it all. Somebody has left you birdie, gotta be an accident. I found you. People are mean, birdie, I know. Mr. Skinner always says so. But it's not that bad, birdie. Will take you home. Be good company for Momma when Luther at the carwash. She'll like you. God, she says, you know, blesses all living things. Even the swear-word people that Mr. Conrad talks about. The assholes and shitheads.

Momma says people like Luther are special. Different. But I don't know. But don't worry birdie, someone knows. Luther don't know too much about all that, but if Luther can come back after Luther dead, Luther want to come back as a white feather birdie. Like you. And you birdie, could come back as a retard. Feed Luther baloney sandwiches. And Mr. Skinner, he's a real donkey he says sometimes. And Momma says she's a silly old goose. And Luther's mad as a hatter she says and laughs so there are lots of other birds and things to come back in. And you know what else, birdie? You know what else? These fingies that are tapping your birdie cage, you know what else? They look like little dancing girls.

22

Dark Leavings

HE STANDS AT THE SPOT. He's survived the Asian hordes. The shitbox had started up against all odds. The nightmare is almost over so what the fuck is happening?

His hands hang open at his sides, palms out, imploring. Paint cans and plank are overturned, the cardboard from B.C. Apples and the grocery bag have been tossed aside. All that's left is a muddy indent the size of a mangled bird cage, the bird and the coop itself, flown.

He stares down, the faces of Katrinna Reticuli and Hector Moses Lake, not too friendly, appearing momentarily in the muddy indent, this sudden vision put down to stress and drinking, boozatanical intakings and nights spent in garbage containers. And, for mercy's sake, is the *kakatoe galerita triton* able to break through metal cages and amble off like a fucking turtle with its home on its fucking back?

Hands, no longer imploring, now grasping, clutching, enveloping the thin necks of weeds and grasses, pulling them out by the roots. The air filled with uprooted flora and fauna, smell of freshly dug earth in a desperate search for that which is not there—a white plume, a bill of sturdy black—one would settle for two eggs on a bed of rotten humus.

He stops. When the eyes and reason fail, conjure lies.

It could be possible that Katrinna Reticuli and Hector Lake have it, returning hours earlier while one lay hidden from the Asian terror. They came back looking, are drawn to the spot by raucous screeching and upward inflections and sit this very minute on one's dead grandmother's sofa, three bundles of the heroin drug less a few caps for personal use scattered over the table.

He brushes himself off, it's six o'clock in the morning. Time to head for home whatever the consequences. And a stop, for sure, at the bootlegger's along the way.

He has the bottle of bootlegged whisky in his left hand. The fist of Hector Lake connects, cleanly, on his right cheekbone. Jerry Lowe staggers back, reaching out with his other hand and grabbing the first heavy object he can find.

Katrinna appears barging past Hector Lake. "Not that! Not my mother's antique clock!"

Jerry Lowe regains his balance holding the bottle outstretched behind him to protect it from Hector Lake.

"Give me the clock, Jerr. Leave him alone, Hector. Let him in."

Hector Lake moves aside, Jerry Lowe coming forward cautiously and handing over the clock to Katrinna. Hector Lake steps back further, nose wrinkling.

"What—"

Jerry Lowe moves more confidently, his squalid condition

holding them at bay. Katrinna replaces the clock and she too backs away.

"Jerry . . ."

"I shit my pants."

"Mmufph."

"But the car's okay ay."

"Ack—"

"And the bird's gone."

"ACK—"

"I will take breakfast on the veranda after cleaning up. No need to lay the table, too pretentious. A simple kitchen unbreakable glass for the whisky, nappies for the cheese. And hold all calls. Feed any of the other guests who wish to eat, I may be awhile. Can't stand on formality. Brush the mare (he looks at Hector Lake) and have the brute in the kitchen take the Afghans for a walk."

He shuffles by, waiting to be jumped. Katrinna presses against the wall to let him pass. And on down the hallway to the bathroom where one may close the door and let fall any last vestige of dignity. And is he angry, or just humiliated? One is on the point of surrender to whatever fate has in the cards, there may be repercussions, there may not.

Now running water into the tub, face planted in front of the mirror. One's left eye is beginning to swell, gently closing. And torn shirt parts are still wrapped about one's head. The bootlegger never said a thing, has seen it all. Leave the turban on, you've earned it. A stiff and aching body lowered into steaming water—Nude Man In Tub With Shirt On Head. Almost as funny as the Banana Peel Man earlier peeking out of a garbage container.

His breath catching. Let out. And swig long and hard from the bottle.

Yeow.

That's better.

A flick-knife pulled from a pocket of the soiled jeans over the side of the tub and laid on the soap ledge beside. Keep this handy, one never knows, does one. Forgot all about it when the shit was coming down back at the lumberyard. Just as well, could have made things a lot worse.

His head resting on the tub rim, warmth rising to and over one's stubbled chin. Exhale deep breaths, ponder an office high in the clouds, one's self at the desk. Seated at the top of the ladder.

Fucking bird.

But something is not right. Don't think about it. Hector Moses Lake and Katrinna Reticuli don't seem too put out, really, taking it all suspiciously well. Didn't get a good look at their eyes but their voices and demeanors did seem a little 'fixated', so to speak. Like they've somehow already scored some stuff and have satisfied their cravings. One has lost the bird, three bundles of heroin. And no one is kicking in the bathroom door about one's ears, pushing one's head beneath the waters. One smack in the eye, that's all.

That's all?

He leaps, like a southern fish dropped in northern waters, hand reaching for the knife at the sudden poundings on the door. Hector Lake can be heard on the other side of the door asking to come in and Jerry Lowe out of the tub remaining ready, reluctant to obey as a puddle forms on the floor.

"Don't be stupid, Lowe. Open the fucking door."

Jerry Lowe moving to unlock it, got to face the music sometime. A jazz refrain probably pounded out on one's head by Hector Lake's fists. Remain standing, though, knife in one hand, bottle in the other. Be prepared to swallow one, throw the other. And for christ's sake don't mix them up.

Hector Lake ducks low, marching in, steering clear of the pants bundled on the floor. A meathook hand drops the toilet seat, the seat crying out as Hector Lake sits, his eyes on the knife.

"For pete's sake, man . . ."

Jerry Lowe back into the tub under a protective blanket of soapy water. It's hard to be assertive when the wang-dang is hanging shrivelled and exposed. Hector Lake running his fingers up and down an old scar on his right forearm.

"What's with the head gear, anyway?"

"It's been a rough night, Hector, and I'm in no mood for bullshit."

"Okay, okay. Sorry about the eye. But what the fuck happened?"

At last. A chance to tell his side. How one had good reason to split the scene that was unfolding under the revolving yellow scallop. Not an act of cowardice. Intended to hide the whacked-out bird, then the shitbox. In case the cops came. And they did. Then went back in good faith to help with the Asian mob, was only using one's head. And narrowly missed a night in the bucket, almost nailed in turn by the Bhindranwale. Hid the night out in an industrial garbage container only to find the bird gone this morning. And thankful at least to be alive and in one piece. And what's more, one is going to finish this bottle then get another, maybe two. That is all. And the smell. Yes, that. It's the smell of shit as one well knows. An unfortunate accident, happens in combat all the time. Makes it easier to run, by the way, freeing much needed muscles and lightening the load.

Tiny ripples lap the sides of the tub. It's a relief that Hector Lake seems amused at least. Jerry Lowe smiles bleakly, but his eyes are wary, knife at the ready under the foam. Still waters run deep, but deeper still the waters of junksick junkies. And it's still not altogether right all this apparent cheerfulness of Hector Lake and Katrinna Reticuli. No cockatoo. No dope. No nothing.

"So, I'm sorry it screwed up, Lake."

Hector Lake on his feet, towering above.

"Don't worry about it. Want another laugh? It was the wrong bird. The Man came by, said he went into the store an hour later to check and the baby cockatoo was still there, over on another wall. But Katrinna and I worked it out. We figured something had gone wrong. Man's coming back with the stuff in about fifteen minutes."

"You worked it out?"

"Yeah. You don't owe us nothing if that's what you're thinking."

"Nope. That's not what I'm thinking."

"Sorry again about the eye. Thought you'd run rat."

"Didn't."

"I know. It's cool."

"Okay, then."

"Had a fullback on the team once. Thought every time we screwed up it was his fault. Had to babysit him through the entire game. Ended up boozing himself to death only a few years later."

"Hmm."

"Hope you don't do that."

"I won't."

"Good. Katrinna worries about it."

"Really."

"She just acts that way. You know, the 'tough broad' bit."

"Yeah. Heart of mush."

"That's right."

"I feel better."

"Good."

"So . . . how'd you guys fix it?"

"Oh, that."

"Yes, that . . ."

Hector Lake ducking low out the door, leaving the words hanging in the air above the bundle of soiled trousers.

"Katrinna put up your sound system as collateral. Man's going to leave us two bundles, anyway."

The soapy waters are now still, like death, cooling. Jerry Lowe is as still as the water but heating up. One has been running off-tackle, as Hector Moses Lake might put it. Hit from the blind side. You have only to make ten yards it's said, for a new chance at another ten. And then another after that and so on until the field, if it ever does, runs out. Interesting game, football. But now the only thing of any value in the whole place is gone. Five-Point-One channel speaker system. Hideaway Acoustimass module. Audio calibration system. A library of CDs and nowhere to play them, no music for god knows how long. And why should he expect anything different, really, this is not a lifestyle that honours personal effects.

At last then able to move, tongue and jaw muscles getting

ready and stoked with full lung capacity and only one word to say.

"KATRINNA!"

Small feet pad outside the door. Katrinna comes in, stopping short at the trousers.

Jerry Lowe sits in the bathtub uneasy again as he's reminded of Katrinna's husband who met his fate in his own bathtub all those years ago.

"Nice hat."

He ignores the comment.

"Is it true?"

"Yes, it's true."

"And all (ack) eight speakers too?"

"That's the deal."

"The DEAL?"

"Get cleaned up. Everything's fino."

Everything's fine.

More words left hanging for him to digest and he's alone again, waterlogged, perhaps a little brain-dead and a choice to drown or face the day with no surround music. A life of petty crime is one way to pass the time, felonious and grim. But it's not going to go on. Changes will be made. Had made a promise to that family on the last B&E with Hector Lake. A big house in West Vancouver and one had inadvertently glanced at a portrait on top of the bureau one was looting—the family done up in ties and blazers, bows and lace—heads shiny wet and mouths dangling white squeaky smiles from faces staring out under studio lights of an 8 x 10 glossy. And you told them. You told them then: "It's an ugly cruel world you poor idiot bastards." And explained there are a million stories in the Naked City, all different, a mishmash of paths out there, dissecting, reticulating, twining and twisting, interlacing the smallest act with the largest. No one is ever acting solely alone, and no one is unaccountable. A fart in Menoza, Argentina, could eventually cause a war in Jiangsu, China. Who knows? And you knew it would be impossible for them to comprehend why they were being robbed, impossible for those shiny faces to understand it was because of things that are none of their business. Or understand that thieves have problems too, like finding something worth taking. In the old days they had the *Narrenschiff*s, ships of fools. An intriguing idea but not practical now, the whole world would be at sea.

There's a pattern on the bathroom ceiling much like the one in the living room, the result of some leakage from the suite above. He can see clouds in it with rust-coloured peripheries. And faces. Even what looks like a man driving a tractor, an old farmer guy towing something through the scrub of the Canadian prairie. A change is gonna come, he thinks. One no longer intends to live this way, no way, baby. Not like Hector Lake and Katrinna Reticuli. Have already plans to start anew, maybe even pay back that student loan. Katrinna and Hector will continue on, skulking in doorways waiting for their connections who will rip them off and vice versa, a mad dark dance of forlorn survival buoyed by spells of welcome oblivion to begin all over again the next icy cold morning, their minds and bodies slowly disappearing until all that's left is the word on the street, "Hey, did you hear about . . ." It will mean a breaking off, huge rifts. A dark leaving.

His mind drifts idly through the last chaotic hours, the clomping of boots along a chain-link fence; the clang of a tire-iron landing. And rounding that corner in the dark, spying one of the Asian guys leaning up against the fence, winded, his fingers entwined in the wire. He'd looked at him, right in the eye. The Asian guy didn't look angry, vengeful, but tired and almost thoughtful. Not a terrorist from the Punjab. More like a local yokel, not mysterious, just a guy caught up in something that was out of his control, or seemed to be. He didn't even shout, just leaned there, hanging on. He looked a lot like—well—he looked a lot like himself, goddamit.

He watches the faucet, one eye now fully closed, the other staring wide. One is alive, isn't one? Wiggle those toes, rotate head. And take another pull of whisky. Keep head tipped back, the one good eyeball to the guy on the tractor. Keep swallowing, something's plugged. Whisky down the gullet, something better happen soon. More. A buzz. YEOW!

That's better.

23

Weaned from Toads

SINGH SIDHU SITS ATOP A STACK of tires in the body shop, on his feet tan Adidas Effigy cross trainers signifying a daytime activity. It's eleven-thirty in the morning and he's brought the Green Behemoth in for repairs as soon as he was able to quit the family house unnoticed. The Fear sits with him, but has strangely diminished in its power. It seems to have been replaced with a number of lesser, more mundane fears, such as the simple fear of one's family, or fear of the cost of repairs for the Green Behemoth. Jagit Sanghera leans against the wall beside him (Nike Air Max Conquer runners) and they watch the blur of sparks as the body man bends over with a rag, lets it plop in a bucket of cloudy water, pulls it out again and lets it drip over the whirring blur as he holds the sander tight against the side of the Green Behemoth. Singh Sidhu shifts his position, his rear still sore from the tumble he took the night before and finding some comfort over the hole of the tire. "Torment in general," he thinks, and it may really be the Indian way. His return home in the wee hours of that morning had only reinforced the notion.

He had dropped off Jagit Sanghera and the brother younger, then drove home through the silent early morning streets. His head hurt, his butt hurt, his pride hurt. He had struggled at the front door of the house, attempting to enter undetected. His sister hears, on her way upstairs with a high-calorie snack swiped from the kitchen in the early morning hours so their parents wouldn't know about it. She stashes the tray in her room and makes for the parents' bedroom ignoring the frantic whispers from Singh Sidhu in the hallway below. The folks are awakened with an urgent warning, that someone is sneaking in, thieves or rapists. And in the hallway below Singh Sidhu, shoes in hand, trying to navigate the black wilderness called home, afraid to turn on a light. Someone has moved the furniture. A stumble into the hall table that only this morning used to be against the opposite wall, Singh Sidhu rattling and clattering in the downstairs hall wanting only that there not be a scene. But the slap of the old man's slippers can be heard approaching overhead as one stands exposed in a wash of light in mid-tiptoe across the front hallway floor, the old man at the top of stairs heading down, nostrils flaring. The old lady appears next, dressing gown barely touching the tops of the steps as she too descends. And then, he's sure, she suddenly leaves the stairway, her body arrowing straight up and coming down in a terrible wind. The tiny family circles about him, sister, mother, father; Singh Sidhu entwined with a bruised head, aching arse, the stink of beer. The old man set to rave but interrupted by Grandma who stands now at the top of the landing, her weak eyes staring down, her voice scratching in her native tongue—"Who is it? Who is it? I know."

And his father answering, "Shut up Mother, go back to bed."

"The drunken Sidhu men have always brought disgrace. Ruffians and madmen."

"Go to bed woman."

"Weaned from toads and brains of cow dung."

"I am coming up to cut out your heart."

"You don't scare me, son-in-law. *Khota*."

"I don't, don't I."

"Black-hearted *balgam*."

And then Mom clutching the old man at the foot of the stairs, the old man clutching the banister making sounds like *Ack, Ack*.

"No, Ragit. She is old."

"I've had enough."

"She's old."

"She's a whore."

"That was long ago."

"*ACK!*"

And he'd maintained a tactful silence in the downstairs hallway still trying not to be noticed as the harangue continued. A diversion, however ugly, may be just what the doctor ordered, the smokescreen one needs. And moving then toward the basement door, they'd lengthened the hallway while he's been gone. Almost to the basement door and the old man seen turning toward him, sister and mother departing quickly back up the stairs to protect Grandma who bangs away on a gong at the top of the landing shouting things about the Sidhu men. The old man then thankfully turning to confront the noisier threat and heading back up the stairs as Singh attains the basement door that leads to his room and pauses, unsure if it's the right thing to do after all, to save one's own ass while Grandma's was in danger.

"I will kill you this time, woman."

"You don't scare me, *mengna*."

"Father, come to bed. Pay her no mind."

"She has defiled enough."

"*Eeeek* he has me."

"Let her go."

"It's the end old woman."

"You can't, Ragit."

"I will."

"He wouldn't dare."

The shop man turns off the sander and looks down at the door of the Green Behemoth. He shakes his head and the sander starts again as Singh Sidhu sees his life in the sparks as they begin to fly and he resolves then not to marry, no matter what, having closed the basement door just as Grandma let go one last insult while hung by the old man by her ankles over the upstairs railing.

> "The
> Sidhu
> men
> have
> water
> in
> their
> veins."

24

Bathtards

SYLVAIN DEACON IS THINKING of the three Asian guys from the night before. He's feeling a little guilty, after all, they weren't really doing anything that appalling, just not that smart. They were more the victims than the perpetrators. The yo-yos in the Volkswagen were the real wackos, although, after all these years of wackos, it was getting harder and harder to separate them from the non-wackos. And it isn't right that he should be thinking of wackos at all, not right now. He was free at last, a couple of weeks to experience sanity and the rare blessing of idleness, and that without guilt.

He presses back into his seat, his long legs sporting a pair of light tan Dockers, his torso an airy shirt of sky and earth colours. He gazes out the window at twenty-nine-thousand feet over a foamy layer of thick white cloud stretching to the curve of the horizon.

He leans to the window. Through a break in the clouds a tiny toy ship is visible making its way below, a white vee fanning out from its tail. In the seat beside, Lucille dozes, her head resting on his shoulder in this, the compartment first class. An olive shudders in the cocktail, through the cabin a brief tremor as the plane floats an air pocket. He is at last away from it all, well almost, as on the movie screen up front George C. Scott soundlessly herds hookers off the streets of L.A. into the paddy wagon while his sidekick Stacy Keach gets his arm caught in the rolled-up window of a car driven by a maniac woman who takes off. He glimpses the car, silently hitting a lamp post and smiles. Just make-believe, just a movie. Stacy Keach rolls along the pavement looking flustered, scared and in pain. Reminds him a bit of Ferg. Hard to believe it was only two days ago he himself was embroiled in the real thing. A body naked on a rooftop, puke smells and dead Chinese kids, out-of-body experiences and a pancake man alone under the stars.

He rubs his belly, soon the white sands, breezes tickling upturned toes. The only complaining in the next few weeks, if any, will be done by himself, a chance to give a little back maybe. The name, my good man, is The Deacons, and this steak which one would never in a million years have dreamt of ordering while back home, is underdone, sir . . . uh . . . *improvident* wouldn't one say. And maybe send back a bottle of wine too just for the hell of it. A frigid stare to the waiter—We are not the rabble, sir, but a vacationing couple who, in their working hours, are in the service of the Queen, and the service in this establishment is nowhere . . . uh . . . *exemplary* enough, sir.

He stretches and cocks his head. Nods to the stewardess. They aren't called that anymore, he remembers. Can't remember the new politically correct term. Good. Who cares, waited on hand and foot so why not indulge, even if you don't really want anything. And time to wonder how

Ferg's doing, a quick goodbye over drinks the night before last and Ferg's eyes had drooped like a Bassett Hound's. "Have a good time, Deac," he'd said. "Do a hula for me. Ha, ha." And just a hint of sadness in that voice, a faint smell of puke still off those shoes. Ferg probably stayed late in the bar, recounting for anyone who'd listen the events of his day. And then would have weaved his way home, a third floor one-bedroom, no one to greet him and collapsing alone onto the bed. Then a night of little or no sleep, tossing on dreams of bullets flying those few months before, poop in one's drawers, no one else there to turn to under the damp writhing sheets, up restlessly while still dark for another hit of scotch, maybe, lights left off and tripping over shoes and magazines, an ashtray probably toppled, eyes staring blankly out the window on the night, a nocturnal animal living like the leopards and tigers.

Another air pocket rattles the compartment and a tiny startled cry goes up from the old lady a few seats ahead. "Rest assured, lady," he thinks, "if a crash is meant to be, dear heart, it's probably meant to be and it's okay."

He closes his eyes.

Twenty-nine-thousand feet below and a hundred and fifty miles north, a nocturnal animal's eyes are wide open, its body crouched low in a hawthorn bush beneath an eastside slum-pit apartment wall. From high out one top window a voice occasionally lisps forth, "Don't come any clother or I'll blow them away!"

Ferguson remains hidden, unsure of his next move, the hawthorn bush prickling his ass. All the assholes are out today, angry harelips and welfare week cannot be things of this world. How wise is it to give money to the poor so they can buy booze and drugs and hold their families hostage? And then call the cops to sort it all out. This dumb fuck up there with no more hope, no more whisky, his only entertainment is pointing a gun at the heads of his family and calling the whole world "bathtards."

He glances back at Stenner and Carp who are huddled down behind the police blue-and-white parked in the alley. Right guys, come check it out. Just like you told me to. Surprised you haven't driven off, gone for a beer.

He hears a short *pop*—christ, that asshole at the top window's now taking potshots. At all the bathtards.

He digs in deeper around the hawthorn bush, feeling the urge to pee. Can't even run for cover. The laundry bills have sky-rocketed these last few months, should have been a baker like the old man. Who ever pissed their pants because the dough didn't rise? He thinks again of the gas station manager, can't get that bozo out of his mind. Looking a lost soul under the gas station lights. Had almost felt sorry for him, what was the name. Partridge? Packer? That poor bastard probably doesn't have all that bad a life, just thinks he does. At least he'll never have to squat in the weeds while under fire praying he will live long enough to get drunk one more night in order to forget the day he's just survived.

Another *pop* and Ferg hears a *THWACK* over his right shoulder. He giggles suddenly, the goofball is firing at Stenner and Carp. Oh lord, what a riot. He thinks of Sylvain Deacon, flying to more peaceful shores. Another shot comes from the window above as he fumbles the switch on his radio. "Liquidator's fucking special . . ."

FOOZLERS

He crouches even lower, hurting himself. An early morning scotch hasn't helped the nerves much. His mouth is dry, his throat feels swollen. A puff of dust is thrown up a few yards to his right, a helpless feeling—the sky has just opened up with a real-life threat, real-life death is in the air in the form of tiny metal projectiles, too small and moving too fast to see, seeking targets. The fear is tangible—another day—just another day and try not to squawk when one calls for help. Try to sound steady and stuff the whole radio down your throat if necessary, to make sure they hear the message, the message for more.

More, you idiots! More back-up . . .

GLOSSARY

KUTTA—dog
TRAKKA HOEA—rotten
MENGNA—ratshit
HARAM DA—bastard
SAJJANIA—friends
SAJJAN—friend
BALGAM—mucus, scum
NASHEBAZ—drunkard
KHOTA—ass
PHARNA—arrest

ACKNOWLEDGEMENTS: Dryden, H.G. Wells, Coleridge, Elizabeth Browning, George Dillon, Julia Carney, Schiller, S.A. Brooke, Mathew Henry, Havelock Ellis, W. Shakespeare, Charles Lamb.

Tom Osborne is the author of *Under the Shadow of Thy Wings*, *9 Love Poems*, *The Reamer's Car Club Blues Band Story* and *Please Wait for Attendant to Open Gate*—the latter two of which are now "rare" finds—and the uncategorizable *Tenth Avenue Bike Race*. Tom was one of the founding editors of the notorious Pulp Press Publishing Co. (now Arsenal Pulp Press) in the '70s. His work has appeared in *Geist, subTerrain,* and *3-Cent Pulp*. He currently lives in Maple Ridge, B.C. *Foozlers* is his first published novel.